Angels Among Us

A collection of short stories

Michael D. Nadeau

Angels Among Us

First paperback edition July 2023 Michael D. Nadeau

Cover design by Michael D. Nadeau
Typography and Interior Design by Michael D. Nadeau

ISBN (paperback) 978-1-960654-00-7

ISBN (eBook) 978-1-960654-01-4

Also from Michael D. Nadeau

<u>The Land of Lythinall Series</u>

The Darkness Returns

The Darkness Within

Tales From Lythinall

The Darkness Falls

<u>Rise of the Archmage Series</u>

Dragon Caller

Dragon Master

Acknowledgments

To my beautiful wife, Sheila, who puts up with me every single day of her life; without her I would be lost in darkness. You inspired most of this—unknowingly—as you lay in that hospital bed fighting for your life. It was during that time that I had this idea of angels walking among us and answering prayers as surely something was looking out for you that year.

I would also like to thank Jason Stokes for starting this whole thing with Gestalt Media's monthly story contest. It inspired me to evolve this whole thing into the massive collection you will now see.

Contents

Act I

Act II

Appendix

Foreword

If you are here for some religious writings of the tenets of your faith...I apologize ahead of time. I'm not trying to mislead anyone; the title is exactly what this book is about. However, the fictional characters that lie herein are not what you probably thought was coming. While I did take some of these characters from the Bible —it doesn't matter which one - so don't ask—I only used their likenesses and known characteristics. I took great liberty with these stories and some of you may or may not have problems with how these characters are portrayed and/or received. That being said, if you like good, uplifting stories, then by all means continue, I promise if that is what you like, then you won't be disappointed. I had fun trying to inspire everyone that reads these stories that there is also hope in the world as well as love, and that everyone can somehow be redeemed. This collection of stories is meant to bring comfort to the reader, despite the recent troubles of the wide world around all of us.

These stories were originally written for a writing contest sponsored by **Gestalt Media Publishing** before they closed their doors; most of these are in their anthology put out in 2021. Like everything else I write, I connected these stories to form one long arc. Inside this book are a couple more bonus stories that intertwine with the others that I had lying around from other submissions. Originally these short stories were kept at three thousand words, but I expanded some of them for this work and a lot of the stories grew in depth and flavor. If you read and liked them before, you will enjoy them even more now.

The world these stories take place in is the very world you set foot in everyday, albeit a changed one from what you may know. On this Earth, humanity ruined what they had and now—in this not-so-distant future—the people have struggled and tried to rebuild. Places like **New Dallas**, **New Seattle**, and the **New England City States** are places where humanity has put themselves together again, having clean streets and a flourishing economy as well as structure and law. These places resemble the old cities here and there with only minimal changes and the people live their lives the way you would think - day to day jobs, work, even playing outside with their kids; yet there are still places that remind humanity what they had done wrong.

Places like **Old Chicago**, **the Ruins of Phoenix**, **Old California Island**, and **Old Miami** are places of crumbling buildings, flooded streets, and abandoned buildings where the less fortunate struggle to survive and cower from bandits and warlords. These places were hit the hardest during the catastrophe and never fully recovered. The people that live in these places are the poor and homeless that could never afford to move to the newly rebuilt cities, or the stubborn that refused to leave their hometowns. Life here is hard; gangs, and even cults, are common place in the darkest shadows of the ruins. People still work and try to live, but the places are crumbling and the conditions deplorable at best. Sickness runs rampant as hospitals are almost non-existent here in the badlands, but there are still places to find solace - mainly refugee camps with blazing red crosses on the sides. Yet all is not lost. Angels and other mysterious beings from our distant past are walking among us, helping when they can and trying to stop others from bringing us back down into chaos. Danger lurks around every corner and you never know who is going to be on your side when the time comes. Lines like black and white are blurred to an even grey in these books, so buckle up—if you're still here—and get ready to dive into a world full of twists, turns, and uplifting tales of Angels Among Us

Act I:

Setting the Stage

"My father belived that humanity could withstand anything that was thrown at it. Now I say to you, let us rebuild and show him he was right!" — Michael Harris. Only surviving son of former president, Richard Harris, two months after the clamity.

THE CASE

He walked down the dark street, the torrent of rain on his worn hat and longcoat drowning out the cars as they drove by. Visibility was almost nil in the heavy deluge, yet he knew where he was going; he had been this way before. Marcus Brant turned a corner and narrowly missed a drenched street walker as she plied her trade to a parked car. She was leaning in through the car's window as the rain soaked her fake furs and even though she was engaged in conversation, she still wiggled her ass as Marcus stumbled by.

They never give up, he thought as he ignored her with practiced ease, put his head down, and pushed on through the downpour. He stopped in front of a non-descript building and looked at the graffiti on the door, smudged and running with the heavy rain; new paint meant someone marking their territory. *Great,* he thought as he opened the heavy door with his shoulder, stumbling inside out of the rain. Marcus had visited this abandoned apartment building more than twenty times since he took this case, yet still he came back expecting a miracle. He shook his hat out as he dripped onto the dirty floor, and stuffed it into his pocket as the water pooled at his feet before snaking off into the dust and grime. Every time Marcus came here, he hoped to find something he missed—something that might possibly lead to that girl's death. Marcus flipped the switch near the door and watched the old lights struggle to brighten; the wiring in the rundown building was older than he was. His nostrils rebelled at the intrusion of smells that assailed them, the blood saturating the room as well as the musk of death that just never seemed to go away after a killing.

Marcus Brant was a private investigator in the great windy city of Chicago. He had seen a lot of weird cases in his forty years on this world, though this one was one for the record books to be sure. Marcus brushed his black hair out of his mismatched eyes—one blue and one hazel— and pulled a cigarette out of his coat pocket. Shaking the water off of his lighter before firing it up, he took a long drag and looked around at the mess. The police had left the caution tape and the chalk outline, knowing that no one would bother to complain about it in this run-down building, never mind this neighborhood. Blood still stained the floor, walls, and even parts of the ceiling in this gruesome scene; piles of vomit from the arriving officers could still be seen on the edges of the walls where they ran to empty their stomachs. Marcus stepped out of the water puddle his long coat had made and took a drag off of the damp cigarette. He tried to imagine who would do something like this and for once in his life he was at a loss.

His client, a Mr. Steven Riley, had hired him to get to the bottom of his daughter Kelly's death. His client didn't believe the police report of gang violence or drugs, so here Marcus was... soaking wet and stumped for the first time in years. He had been over this crime scene dozens of times, in the light of day to the evening nights. He hadn't found anything of consequence or even out of the ordinary, which made the whole thing even worse, mainly because he didn't believe it either. The only clues the police had found were an odd pamphlet for some obscure church and residue of cocaine. The dead girl's wounds were caused by a knife—over forty stab wounds to the chest, legs, and face—and of course there were no witnesses. That pretty much wrapped up the case, though deep in his gut he knew that something was off. Marcus had looked into the dead girl's history and found absolutely no traces of prior drug use, no friends that hung out with known drug sellers, not even a parking ticket. When the father said she was clean, he wasn't kidding; if someone was dirty, Marcus could find out.

"You back again, Marcus?" an unsteady voice asked from a broken-down cardboard box in the darkened corner. The building may have been an apartment complex in the past, but now it was just an empty husk.

"Sure am, Vincent. How's the cough?" Marcus asked, walking over and handing the old man a smoke. "Are you staying dry tonight?" Marcus had let the old man in five nights ago when he had found him soaked and shivering in the adjacent alleyway. He knew the police would kick the old man out eventually, but that would take some time.

Vincent hawked up a lung answering the first question and spit into an old coke can. "Dry as a bone. This box is great and I have no need to go out in that monsoon tonight. I even got me my dinner last night." The old man, who had to be in his seventies at the very least, held up a half-eaten sub, still in its deteriorating wrapper. "I ate some last night and saved the rest for tonight."

"Great. Hey, anyone come around since Monday?" Marcus always asked, just in case. It had been two days since he had checked the place out and you never knew when lady luck would shine down on you.

"Actually, yes."

"Really?" Marcus had walked away but turned back at the statement. He expected the same answer he always got. Nothing. "What did they look like? Did you get a name?" He couldn't hide the excitement in his voice.

"It was a young girl handing out more of those weird pamphlets," Vincent answered, fishing around in his bag and holding up a piece of crumpled paper in the air. "She never gave no name, nor even asked mine. Here, she gave me one and said it would change my life if I was still here Friday. You can have it."

Marcus took the crumpled paper and unfolded it, shaking out dry crumbs of Vincent's leftover sandwich. He looked the pamphlet over, scrutinizing every word. It was identical to the one found near the body. Originally the police thought it was already here; trash left in the abandoned building. Kelly was a devout catholic and wasn't one to explore other religions, but this changed things; another identical pamphlet meant a clue. "Thanks, Vincent, you keep your eyes out and if there's any trouble you scoot all right?"

"I'm too old for trouble Marcus; I would just sleep through it anyway."

Marcus laughed and pulled his hat out of his wet pocket and slipped in on with a shiver as water fell down his back. He walked to the door, stuffing the pamphlet into his coat, and smiled. He only ever got to look at the original once, as the police had put it into evidence right away as standard procedure, but now he had his own copy to scrutinize. Marcus opened the door to the driving rain and ducked out. He was soaked in seconds, the wind almost taking his hat off despite the hand holding it. He would go home and get some rest before digging into this church pamphlet, but at least now he had a lead.

THE CHURCH

The next day Marcus woke up to his blaring alarm and struggled off of the couch. He had crashed at his office last night after a long day and it seemed easier to get an early start. He grabbed some coffee to wake up and sat down at his computer to do some research on this church. When he took the case, he had looked it up from what he could remember, yet with the girl's background in her religion, he too had discarded the information as happenstance. Now, as he kicked himself for dropping the ball, he clicked away on his laptop, bringing up the obscure church that had been recruiting members with pamphlets with the website on the bottom of the paper. *At least they weren't handing out white robes and cool aid*, he thought as he waited for his slow internet to load the page.

The Church of the Northern Crown, located right here in Chicago, had a very dark and foreboding website displaying images of demon horns and blood-stained crosses. Marcus wrote down the address of the church—the feeling of deepening dread only getting worse—and kept scrolling. Marcus read up on the tenets of the church and what they offered to the people that joined. It wasn't until the bottom of the page that the name given to their patron rang all sorts of alarms in his sleep-addled brain. Belial was their god and the writing actually made the hair on his arms stand up.

The Worthless One, craver of lust and pain, shall be your guide in this world of flesh. Let him guide you in your choices and ever you will be rewarded with a place at his side when He comes. Bring others into the fold so that He may grow strong and soon He will be set free.

Marcus opened a new tab and typed in the name *Belial*. He hadn't been to church since he was eleven; it just wasn't something he ever bothered with. Yet, he had always been fascinated with demons and knew most of their names by heart; this one was very familiar. The page loaded and he skimmed the contents. *Oh crap,* he thought. *I hate being right.* The first thing he found was an entry in some satanic reference.

Belial means "No master" and symbolizes independence and rewarding personal accomplishment. Belial represents the earth and all who crave carnal pleasure upon it. It is said that he fell to earth following Lucifer's fall from Grace, becoming one of the first demons upon the world.

He clicked another entry and cold fingers dragged slowly down his spine; it just got worse from there. Belial was a champion of simply being human, the desires of the flesh, the gain of material wealth, and the carnal pleasure we all pursue. In essence, do what you want regardless of the consequences. These fanatics had the perfect front to do whatever they wanted in the name of some ancient demon that didn't even exist. It was paradise to most people nowadays and they would flock to this if it gained momentum.

"What was a good girl from Goshen, Indiana doing with Satanists in Chicago?" Marcus stood and walked around his office, talking to himself. It was his process to work out clues. "Okay, let's go through what I have," he said, walking to his board and taping the pamphlet up with a string. "Kelly moves here two months ago with her boyfriend then leaves him and moves into a one-bedroom apartment a month later. She affords this on a waitress's pay, yet can afford to eat out at fancy restaurants every week." Marcus wrote the name Belial on the pamphlet and led another string to the apartment building. "If the first pamphlet was hers, maybe she was given one, like Vincent? Told to meet there? But why was she killed?" Marcus stepped back and looked at the board from a distance, trying to see any semblance of a pattern. When he saw what he had added his skin crawled with fear, those cold fingers now gripping his spine and holding it fast; it was a pentagram.

Kelly's apartment, the abandoned building, the church, the restaurant she frequented, and the first apartment she had with the boyfriend all made a five-pointed star across the city. Worse ... Marcus's office was dead center in all of it.

The blaring ring of his telephone made him jump a good five inches off the ground, his heart thundering in his chest. He stared at the landline sitting on his desk for a good six rings before getting the nerve to pick up the receiver, an unknown fear making him hesitate. He didn't trust cell phones, even though he had one. He much preferred the old landlines whenever possible. Finally, he grabbed it and took a deep breath. "Marcus Brant, P.I."

"Mister Brant, its Steven Riley. Is there any news on the case this week?"

Marcus breathed a sigh of relief at the sound of Kelly's father on the other end of the phone. *What? Did I expect a demon to be calling me?* He cleared his throat before answering the man, feeling a weird tingling in his spine as the dread subsided. "There is indeed, Mister Riley. That pamphlet has turned up again so I'm following up on that church."

"You can't possibly think Kelly would've had anything to do with those blasphemers." The man's voice had turned to acid in a heartbeat, almost stumbling over the words; the man was seething at the idea of his girl straying from the righteous path.

"I'm very thorough, Mr. Riley. If it is a lead, I'll follow it."

"Yes, I know," the man spat over the phone, "It's printed on your business card."

Marcus could hear the man's labored breathing and waited for a minute for him to calm down. "Listen, Steven, I just want to find your daughter's killer. If these people know anything, I'll find out, trust me." Marcus sat down in his chair, letting the man process this, and then continued. "Now, is there anything you could possibly think of that would connect them with Kelly or her boyfriend?"

"Michael? I've never met the young man." Mr. Riley paused, the line crackling with static for a brief second. "She left *him*, didn't she?"

"Yes, but he may have had ties to these people that we can't see. I've looked him up already, dug into his past, yet I may have missed something trivial. Did they ever argue about religion?" Marcus thought it was a long shot, but he never did find a reason for Kelly to break it off with her boyfriend. In all honesty, he never needed to before now; now everything seemed connected.

"Now that you mention it, she did have an argument with her boyfriend about a horn the young man bought online, but I don't know why."

"Thank you, Mr. Riley. I'll look into that as well. I will call later with anything I find.

"No need," Mr. Riley said with a much softer tone. "I'll call again next week and see what you've found. Good luck Mr. Brant." The line clicked and went quiet.

Marcus hung up the phone and sat down, looking at the board once more from his chair. It was already almost noon and his head hurt. He opened the drawer to his right and pulled out an almost empty bottle of whiskey. Marcus would need another bottle of something strong very soon to get through this case. *Looks like I'm sleeping here again tonight,* he thought as he poured himself a glass of whiskey. *Cause I'm going to be here for the rest of the afternoon digging.* This case was getting stranger every minute.

The Precinct

Marcus drank the rest of his whiskey as he looked up various things - Michael, his purchases, anything that may set off a bell in his head. That night he slept fitfully, even with the alcohol running in his system. In the morning he stumbled to his desk to get his pack of dwindling smokes and noticed the door to his office was wide open. Marcus froze with the drawer half open, knowing that even with the whiskey in his blood he had locked the door last night. A shadow to his right alerted him to trouble and he dropped down into his chair as a man swung a bat over his head. Marcus punched out, catching the assailant in the crotch, doubling the man over just as another man came at him from the open door.

"This is what happens to guys who can't leave well enough alone," the second man said, swinging a crowbar with two hands. The metal caught Marcus's shoulder and spun him into the first man, who grabbed him. They took turns hitting the private investigator, mostly in the back and shoulders.

Marcus curled up, feigning helplessness as the guy let him drop, and took several hits as he fought to stay conscious. Five hits, six, and then another before he reached for the bottom drawer and pulled it open. He grabbed his .38 caliber and fired once, then again, the assailants falling back, clutching bloody wounds. Marcus groaned and tried to sit up, reaching for the phone on the desk. He fell back on the floor, dragging the telephone with him as he did, trying to block out the pain. In his haze, Marcus saw one man stumble down the hallway as he dialed 911.

A few hours later he was sitting in the fifteenth precinct, his arm in a sling and bruises on his back, giving his statement.

"In trouble again, Brant?" a familiar voice asked walking up behind him. The man wore a nice suit; his blond hair cut collar length.

"Detective Arnhem. How is the family?" Marcus asked, smiling through the pain.

"They're good. Listen, Marcus, why aren't you at the hospital? I heard these guys you pissed off roughed you up pretty damned good." The detective nodded to the officer at the desk, shooing him away. He sat down and looked over the computer screen, shaking his head. "You're still looking into that girl's death?"

"I'm getting paid to, John," Marcus replied, leaning in and lowering his voice. "Listen, you know what it means when they come after you like this...I'm getting close to something. This girl's death wasn't a drug bust gone bad."

"Or it could be that the drug cartel is coming after you because you're still digging." The detective sighed and crossed his arms, leaning back in the chair. "I know you won't leave this alone, but I think you need to be careful. The guy in your office didn't die so there is no wrongful death we have to look into; I know, self defense," the detective said holding up his hand before Marcus could say anything. Detective Arnhem clicked some keys on the keyboard, finishing the report. "I can stall any investigation for a couple days, so get through the rest of this day and the weekend without getting yourself killed, huh?"

"You got it, John. Thanks again." Marcus got up and left to figure out this horn. He knew right where to start, but first he needed some smokes and to ditch this sling. It wouldn't do to let his enemies know he was hurt.

He went out and got in his car, slamming the door closed so it stayed closed, and pulled out into the street as the radio babbled on about politics. Usually, he liked to hear about the news, but with this case he was just too preoccupied.

"The president talked today about the recent border skirmishes in Korea ..." Marcus hit the radio and changed the station, finding some soft rock for background noise as he thought. He pulled out a piece of paper he had grabbed from his desk before the medics took him out of his office to check him out and looked at it as he drove; it was the young kid's address and the address of the bank the kid

worked at; he could be there in an hour, after he got his smokes and stuff, of course.

THE HORN

By noon, Marcus was in his beat-up sedan in front of an apartment with a new pack of smokes. Michael Vance had moved here after his break up with Kelly, supposedly working at the bank four blocks from here. However, when Marcus showed up at the bank, there was no Michael, even though he was scheduled. Nor was the young man at home, as several knocks and even a severe pounding had proved. So, Marcus sat here on his stakeout and waited, jamming to soft rock and wishing his coffee hadn't run out.

As Marcus lit another cigarette, he saw Michael come around the corner, two bags of groceries in his arms. The kid was dressed in jeans and a leather jacket—by no means bank attire—and bobbing his head to some intangible music only the kid could hear. Marcus got out of his car and slammed his side into the door to close it. He hurried across the street, his longcoat flying behind him in the wind, dodging cars as they blared their horns at him. "Michael? Michael Vance?"

"Mr. Brant?" Michael slowed down - confusion written all over his face. "What can I do for you?" The young man kept walking up his steps, looking back as he unlocked his door, balancing the bags in one arm.

"Can I come in? I would like to talk with you some more about Kelly." Marcus noted that the kid didn't look nervous at all, yet there was still something there; he couldn't put his finger on it though.

The kid froze halfway into his apartment, then hurried in. "Come on in then. What better way is there to ruin my day then a good rehashing?"

Marcus dropped his cigarette on the steps and ground it under his heel. He followed Michael into the apartment, making their way to the kitchen. Leaning against the counter, Marcus took his hat off and dropped it on the counter. "So, I know we've gone over everything before ..."

"Yes, we have," Michael interrupted his voice a bit harsh.

"...but something has come up that I need to figure out." Marcus knew that the kid was aggravated; he just wanted to get back to his life, however shady that may be at the moment. "Did you two fight over something you bought on the internet? Maybe a horn of some sort?"

Michael laughed, closing the fridge and turning around with a curious look in his eyes. "The horn? That's your big lead?" The kid stomped off to his bedroom, muttering under his breath. He came back a minute later with a receipt, crumpled and stained by what Marcus hoped was coffee. "Here, I sold it after she left to some church freak."

"What was the fight about?" Marcus asked, taking the paper and reading it over. It was a handwritten receipt for over two thousand dollars. *Whoa, expensive instrument.*

"She was pissed that I bought some 'devil horn', as she called it. Crazy girl actually cited Bible passages to me, picked it up like it might burn her, then threw it at me." Michael opened the fridge and grabbed a beer, popping the top off on the countertop. "When I made a wise crack about Jesus always forgiving people, she stormed out."

"Wait, this wasn't some sort of instrument? You actually bought some fake demon horn?" Marcus couldn't believe what some people would buy. *Yet for that much money why get rid of it afterwards?*

"Hey it seemed really cool and I thought it would look awesome on my wall." Michael took a pull of off his beer and finished putting the groceries away.

"Did you guys ever make up?" Marcus asked as he looked at the receipt once more trying to see if there was anything he could use from the receipt. "I mean if you sold it..."

"Nope, that was the last time I saw her. Her father came and got her stuff the next day. I sold the horn mainly because it brought up bad memories of her. Before the horn incident I really thought she might be *the one.*"

"Wait ...her father?" Marcus looked up from the receipt to question the kid about that when he noticed a weird shadow on the ceiling. *Just a trick of the light,* he thought cramming the receipt into his pocket for later. "Her father drove all the way from Goshen, Indiana to get her stuff?" Marcus had a bad feeling suddenly. *Why would Mr. Riley lie about meeting the kid?*

"I guess so. He and I didn't sit down and gab about the weather or anything." Michael took a swig of beer and walked to the living room. "Her father did say that she was distraught over the whole thing and that I could try calling her once I sold the horn, but it was too late..."

"All right, Michael, thank you." Marcus put his hat on and walked towards the door. "I'll call you if I think of anything else." Crossing the street, Marcus pulled out his cell phone and dialed the Riley house. He had an older cell phone but it served its purpose when he needed it. He still favored the old-fashioned land lines and stubbornly refused to upgrade.

"Hello?" a feminine voice answered.

"Hello, is this Mrs. Riley?" Marcus asked. "Susan Riley? It's Marcus Brant."

"Oh hello, Mr. Brant, What can I do for you?"

"I was actually looking for Mr. Riley. Is your husband home?"

The silence stretched on for a minute before the woman's voice came back trembling. "Is this some sort of joke, Mr. Brant?"

"No... I...Why do you ask that?"

"My husband died last month, just three days after hiring *you*," Susan said as her voice broke, sobs coming over the line.

Marcus held his phone in his own trembling hand and hung up as he neared his car. *Then who the hell has been calling me on the phone?*

"Mr. Brant!" Michael called from across the street. He was running down the steps towards him. "I thought of something else that might help." Whatever the young man was going to say, however, was lost when a moving truck hit him at full speed.

Marcus stared in horror as the truck just kept going, the body of Michael Vance broken and bloody in the street. His instincts kicking in, Marcus looked at the truck, then the plate, and memorized them. His blood turned to ice when he realized the name of the company the truck belonged to; Northern Crown movers. He rushed to the kid's side to see if the kid had been lucky somehow, but felt no pulse as he bent down and felt the bloody neck. People were filling into the street now, calling the police and crowding around. Marcus looked back at Michael's apartment and swore that he saw that shadow again, sliding across the brick like a slow-moving cloud. Sirens brought him out of his trance and he shook his head to clear it. Nothing about this case was adding up and it was just getting weirder.

THE TRAIL

Marcus found himself at the precinct once more, filling out a report. He looked around for Detective Arnhem but for once the man's intrusive laughter wasn't heard. "Hey, is John in today?" he asked the officer taking his statement—an officer named Davis.

"Oh man. I'm sorry. You haven't heard?"

"Heard what?" Marcus had a sinking feeling.

"Detective Arnhem had a stroke this afternoon. They took him to the hospital and they say he's finally stable."

Marcus sat there in shock, the events of the whole day finally weighing on him. He filled out his report and left, his steps quickened to his sedan. *Calm down Marcus, it's just a coincidence,* he thought as he drove to the abandoned building. It was six-thirty and he had enough time to get a better description of that girl handing out pamphlets from Vincent. He didn't at first because he honestly didn't expect the paper to go anywhere.

Marcus raced down the busy streets, trying to forget about the mysterious deaths surrounding the case. It seemed everyone that he talked to about it ended up dying. *That is impossible. Isn't it?* he thought, glancing in his rear-view mirror at a red light. A black shadow with bright red eyes was staring back at him from his back seat. Marcus screamed and shouldered the door open, falling into the street. He leapt to his feet and drew his revolver—finally carrying it for the first time in over five years because of the attack in his office. Car horns blared at him as the light turned green, but he ignored then as he opened the back door to reveal...no one else in the car. Looking around he finally climbed back into the car and looked in the mirror once more, seeing nothing out of the ordinary. *Losing it man...you're losing it.* Marcus pulled up to the building, parking at the corner as he always did, and got out, eyeing the sky as it darkened.

"Storm coming, handsome, you need a place to stay dry?" a deep, feminine voice asked.

Marcus turned to see the same streetwalker as the other day leaning on the trunk of his car, shaking her ass and giving him come hither eyes. *They really do not give up.* Ignoring her, he walked toward the door of the building and stopped when he saw it was ajar. That sinking feeling settling in his stomach once again, Marcus rushed in, pulling his gun and leveling it to fire. The smell hit him first as he looked around at the bloody scene. Vincent was strung up in the center of the room, his chest cavity open and empty. Blood still dripped slowly from his open body, pooling in the grime and filth below. Vincent's eyes were gone, the empty sockets staring at Marcus with unerring blame.

Gagging and trying not to empty his own insides on the floor, Marcus stumbled out of the building and into the street, just as the rain started coming down. "Damnit!" he swore, scaring the prostitute as he kicked the side of his car door and got in. He knew that he would have to call the police yet again. It looked bad, even he knew that, and they would start to point fingers in his direction at this point. Marcus drove off and stopped at the corner gas station, knowing that they had one of the rare phone booths left in the city. He placed the call anonymously then drove to his office, trying not to think about Vincent's fate. The trail of bodies was adding up quickly now and he needed to rethink things before rushing off.

By eight o'clock that night he was in his office, pacing in front of his board, more string and notes covering the surface. He had looked up the truck company and ran the plates—thanks to one of his contacts in the Chicago Police department. He also looked up the death of Steven Riley and his wife was telling the truth, except Mr. Riley had been calling him regularly as the weeks went on. "What is going on here?" Marcus asked out loud, circling the father's name on the board. "Add the fact that any of the people helping me with this case keep being killed mysteriously and it starts to sound even more insane."

He spun around and drew his weapon as his door opened, his shaking hand holding the weapon that he hardly ever touched until yesterday. The door stood open with no one coming in. "Who's there?" Marcus asked, backing up and getting a better vantage spot. "Come in slowly."

A man walked in with halting steps, obviously wounded. One hand held up in the air while the other cradled bandages to his stomach, the man looked almost sad. It was the assailant that had gotten away after being shot. "Mr. Brant, it's time to come with me."

"Why would I do that?"

"He knew you would ask that. Answer the phone." The man smiled, pointing to the landline on the desk. It rang loudly in the silence, its clarion call echoing down the hall.

Keeping the gun trained on the man with his unsteady hand, Marcus picked up the receiver and held it to his ear, never taking his eyes off the wounded man. "Marcus Brant P.I."

"Mr. Brant, It is Officer Davis. I just wanted you to know that John passed away tonight. I knew you guys were friends so..."

Marcus hung up the phone before the man could continue with the depressing details that would only bring more pain, fear clutching his spine; Marcus knew he had been led by the nose on this the entire time. "Lead the way."

The Meeting

Marcus followed the man downstairs to the street and a waiting black four door SUV. *It couldn't get any more cliché than this,* he thought as the man opened the back door for him. Marcus eschewed a seatbelt in case he had to make a hasty break away and tried to watch as the scenery went by. They were headed for the city limits and towards the outlying countryside. By the time the SUV pulled up, it was pitch black out, with the storm clouds covering what moonlight there was. The rain continued pouring down as it had off and on for the last couple days as they pulled up to an abandoned church, the crumbling stone telling the private investigator all he needed to know; this place was condemned and no one would be looking out here.

"You bring all your dates here, handsome?" Marcus asked the man, trying to goad his guide into giving something away.

"Laugh all you want, Mr. Brant. You will find your answers are waiting inside." The man got out and opened the door for Marcus with a slight bow, his arm still in a sling.

"It's all right; I'll tell them you were gentle." Marcus walked up to the church, noticing that the door was only a piece of plywood with spray paint on it. *Well at least they're as broke as I am,* he thought as he pushed it open and went in. A wealthy cult could do more damage to the masses; these guys didn't even have enough for a real door.

As he entered the building, Marcus saw a group of robed and hooded figures, with a small blond girl in the center, sitting in a chair. Her white shirt—drenched from the rain—stuck to her and revealed a little too much as she lay there writhing in either ecstasy or pain; Marcus couldn't tell because of the gag they had on her. The girl's face was covered in blood and her shorts seemed torn right up the side. "All right - nobody move!" Marcus yelled, drawing his weapon. He muscled through the crowd and got to the girl's side, removing the gag with one hand as he pointed his gun at the various hooded figures around them. "I'll get you out of here, miss."

The girl deftly grabbed his gun and twisted it, wrenching it out of his hand as she slipped off the table and stood. "Take him," she commanded to the robed figures, which lunged forward as one and hammered Marcus with their fists and feet. Soon, the sweet embrace of darkness took him and as he faded, he swore he heard her laughing.

Marcus awoke sometime later. How long he had no clue, yet he could tell it was still dark outside through the broken windows. He was bound and gagged—sitting in the same chair—and the circle now included symbols and a pentagram just like his board. The robed figures had their hoods down and stood a respectful distance from the white outline of the pentagram.

"Welcome, Mr. Brant. We've waited a long time to get you here," the blond girl said as she made her way through the robed figures. She was now dressed in her own robes, albeit a little fancier and trimmed in gold. She motioned to him and someone took out his gag. "Sorry for the gag, it was to prevent you from screaming upon waking...I have a terrible headache."

"Why did you kill those people?" Marcus had to keep her talking until he figured out how to get loose; they had him tied up really tight.

"They were killed to lure you into our trap, of course." She laughed at the face he made and continued. "You see it's right on your business card—*Marcus Brant P.I. I'm very thorough. If it's a lead, I'll follow it.*"

"You could've just asked me here."

"No, I couldn't. Its part of the rules, you see. You have to come here of your own free will, knowing that you could be harmed." She toyed with a dagger, curved and bejeweled, spinning it in her hands. "We needed you...well, He needed you; your body to be exact."

"You're really trying to sell me the demon shtick still?" Marcus asked, wondering how all these people could fall for this kind of scam.

"All will be revealed, Marcus," a man said, lowering his hood. The man looked just like Stephen Riley! "Ah, I see from your face you've heard of my death. This body used to be the man you knew, but now I wear it as a coat; yet it isn't perfect." The man who used to be Steven rolled up a sleeve, showing a black rot crawling up the arm, the flesh starting to flake off in places.

Now that he saw that, Marcus could also see the edges of a darkness blotting the man's neck and forehead, like plague setting in and spreading. " So where do I come in?" Marcus almost had his hands free from the rope he was tied with, just a little more and he could try...something. What that was, he wasn't sure yet.

"You, Marcus, are the perfect host for our lord and master, Belial." The blond walked forward now, twirling the dagger with a gleam in her eye. "Ironically, you're perfect for hosting the great demon because of your condition."

"What condition?"

"Your eyes, Mr. Brant," The mouth of Stephen Riley said. The voice sounded almost...hungry.

"All I have is Heterochromia," Marcus said not understanding any of this. He had always had it, ever since he was a child. His eyes were each a different color; one blue eye and one hazel eye.

Steven laughed and walked forward, a slight limp showing as he did. "Are you familiar with the 'Eyes are windows to your soul' phrase?" He didn't wait for Marcus to answer. Instead, he nodded to the blond girl. She stepped up and unceremoniously rammed the dagger into Marcus's stomach all the way to the hilt. "Never mind if you haven't, Mr. Brant, I assure you it is very true. The eyes are what hold that soul in you, anchoring it. When you die and the life goes out of your eyes, it releases that soul. Your condition is the only one strong enough to anchor my spirit to this plane without rotting away - the only thing that could hold a fallen angel's essence."

"You...drew me here...with bread crumbs..." Marcus said, feeling the life drain out of him slowly. *How did I miss all this?*

"Yes, we did. If Michael had lived, he would've told you that the horn he had was one of a set. A matching set." The man who used to be Mr. Riley pulled out the horn and affixed it to his head with an audible snap, the room distorting slightly as he did. He did the same with a second one, then his form blurred, becoming horrible to behold. He was nine feet tall, with those gruesome horns sticking out of a canine, demonic face with large teeth dripping with what appeared to be blood, yet it seemed more like a spirit than a body.

I'm dreaming, yeah that's it...I'll wake up in my office with a hell of a hangover. His thoughts spun as he faded fast, falling over onto his side, the blood pouring out of his stomach. *Well, I guess I'm not dreaming*, he thought as he fought to get his arms free. It was no use; he had no strength left. He had been led into this, and all those people died. He looked up into the face of the demon and then everything went black. *I'm sorry Kelly...John, Vincent.*

The End

The man who used to be Marcus Brant walked down the street, his new body feeling healthy and whole for the first time in millennia. The being that was Belial smiled at a streetwalker and gave her a hundred-dollar bill, letting her lead him into the darkened alley she was crouched by. Yes, this new body would serve him just fine in this corrupt world and his followers would appease his will whenever he needed them to. He had fallen from heaven a very long time ago, serving Lucifer and his stupid revolt, and, unlike his other brothers and sisters, he and his other brother, Nergal, had lost their body when they did. Now, though, it was his time to lead.

Belial took his fill of the girl's flesh, then consumed her soul, draining it out through her brown, lifeless eyes. He was back in his full power and nothing would stop him this time. The fallen angel never noticed the people on the street all looking to the sky and pointing, nor did he seem to see them all start to run and scream in panic; until it was too late, that is. The shockwave hit hard, blasting mortar and bricks everywhere and sending even his powerful body rolling.

I just got this body, Christ burn in Hell, he thought as he hit hard against a metal dumpster. He leapt up and into the dumpster for protection and held on tight. When he got out of this someone was going to pay dearly. He opened the top to peak at how bad it was outside when a groan from above made him look up. The entire side of the building was coming down right on top of him. The man that used to be Marcus Brant ducked and pulled the top down quickly as everything came down at once. Some days you just couldn't win.

Faces of Evil

THE CHASE

The man walked steadily behind his victim, his gait that of a relaxed stroll more than a hunter after his prey. Nothing about him was what it seemed, even the fact that he looked like a man. His robes were ancient and outdated, seeming more akin to a medieval play than what one would wear on a hot summer night in Miami. Various charms and adornments clattered against his side as he walked, swinging by their own gruesome hangings from chains around his waist. There were bags, a box, dozens of individual keys, even what resembled thin masks.

He wore a wide brimmed hat, pulled low so that the evening shadows played at hiding his features, which was a blessing to all he passed anyway; his true face could send most humans into catatonic states. He stopped at a busy intersection—the bent traffic poles had only a couple working lights that swung on rusty hinges—and chuckled to himself as his quarry turned down a side street. *They always take side streets...*

"Hey, mister, got any change?" a voice asked next to him.

The fallen angel, Nergal—for that was who he truly was—turned and held out his gnarled hands. Each one sporting wicked looking nails that resembled claws more than fingers. He offered them palm up, showing the man that they were empty, then tucked them away once more at his sides. It mattered not that he showed anyone his claws, humans were remarkable at not seeing what was right in front of them, especially since they broke the world. His face, though, was something else entirely. When an angel fell from Grace, they actually lost their wings, and their bodies sometimes melted away or deformed. Others changed completely, their bodies adapting, but they were the minority. His fall had destroyed his body completely, like his brother Belial, but he was able to possess others to use their bodies. One side effect of this, however, was the faces would always turn monstrous almost immediately, as well as the bodies wearing out, giving in to a black rot after too long. So, he had taken to wearing the faces of his victims to blend in and taking a new body every few years.

"S'ok man. What's your name?" The older man asked while waiting for the walk sign to light up, letting him know it was safe to cross.

Nergal smirked under the brim of his hat. He knew what humanity had labeled the fallen angels that survived all those eons ago. They had been called demons and most of them even had horns fashioned out of the burnt useless wings they had once loved. He had used many names and faces over the millennia, though his favorite was gained in an unfortunate swine incident with that holier-than-thou son of God. In fact, he loved twisting the name around sometimes just to have fun with it. "Geonil," the fallen angel answered, giving the name he was using these days.

"That sure is a fancy name. It must be French, right?" The man swaggered into the street as the flashing walk sign lit up and the light turned red for the coming traffic, yet he had crossed paths with a being that many never walk away from untouched.

Nergal waved his hand, changing the traffic lights from red to green, and turned away as cars sped through the intersection once more, running the man down. The body rolled gruesomely over and over until struck by another car. The Fallen angel didn't care to see the old man's fate; he was just having fun. He turned the corner onto the side street as the sound of screeching brakes and a cacophony of shattered glass and metal filled the background, and spotted the man he had marked as his. Nergal had marked this particular target for the rare eye color that he possessed—one blue eye and one hazel eye. Humans called it Heterochromia and it was the one thing that would stabilize a body for him to possess and keep forever. He was hoping it would help with the face thing too, but he wasn't sure. Besides, he had never seen anyone with eyes like this before in all his long centuries on this earth.

The fallen angel fingered the thin masks dangling at his side as he walked on behind his prey. They were the faces of his victims, preserved so that he could wear them and blend into society to sow dissent and havoc. When he wore someone else's face, it only lasted about a year or so, then he had to assume a new face. This is why he kept a collection and switched them out every few months or so as not to deteriorate one completely, but he was running low. When one wore out his true nature started to leak through...like now.

The man he was tailing started to walk faster, finally sensing that he was being followed. Nergal increased his own pace, smiling his wicked grin through long, broken teeth; he *so* loved the chase. His prey turned a corner and the fallen angel followed, only to be caught off guard a second later by the young man standing his ground. With the light behind him, Nergal couldn't quite make out the man's face, but he could tell the stance he had taken; a fighting stance if he had ever seen one.

"Who sent you?" the young man finally asked, his voice loud and confident. The sun had all but disappeared now and the street lights were flickering to life in the humid southern air.

Taken aback by the man's bravado, Nergal hesitated before answering. *Was this man being stalked by someone else?* "No one sent me, young one; I was following you of my own accord." The fallen angel brought his hands out and was about to grab the man when a woman's voice sounded from behind him, stalling his actions and laying bare the trap he had walked into.

"We know."

The Confrontation

Nergal turned to see a girl dressed in all black holding a decanter, her raven-colored hair falling into her face. She tossed the decanter at him, emptying the container's contents—holy water—into his face. He backed up from them both and smiled a wicked grin; they didn't know what he really was.

The man took out a dagger and crouched low, obviously trying to figure out what had gone wrong. "That should've worked, Maria," the man said looking to the woman.

"Why didn't it, Joseph?"

Nergal could now see the man named Joseph—his different colored eyes blazing with controlled fury. The man had a long beard and a rosary hung from his neck. "You think to vanquish me?" Nergal asked them both, his voice almost laughing at the absurdity of the feat.

The woman dropped the empty decanter and pulled a wooden cross out from the folds of her black outfit. "We've banished little demons like you before, monster, tell us your name and be done with it."

"And which cultist summoned you," the man added.

They truly don't know whom they're hunting, Nergal thought as he lifted up his face to look at them directly, pushing up the brim of his hat. Their eyes went wide as his withered flesh and burnt eyes penetrated their sanity. "Foolish mortals, I am no *little* demon." He surged forward and knocked the cross from the woman's hand—accepting the slight burn on his clawed hands as he did so—and slashed her throat with his other hand. That symbol really did work against him, but that was about all that did; holy water had no effect what-so-ever. The cross however, when held by conviction, was painful enough. The woman staggered backwards, clutching at the gaping wound on her neck as the man cried out in horror and shock. "Those little demons you speak about are nothing compared to the likes of me. I am far older than those malevolent spirits created by the fires of Gomorrah."

"Bastard! Tell me your name!" The man cried out as he lunged, stabbing Nergal high in the shoulder. The blade sunk in deep and stuck fast.

Crying out in shock and pain, Nergal swatted the man with a back hand. The blow sent the man tumbling through the air crashing down among the nearby boxes and crates. He rushed over and stepped on the man's chest as his victim tried to stand. "No one *summoned* me, fool; I have been here for an eternity." His foot slid up to the man's neck and he applied more pressure. "You want my name, holy man?" When the man grunted and tried to nod his head, Nergal laughed. "Fine you shall have it, for all the good it will do you. Only one man was ever able to cast me out and you are not Him." Nergal took his foot off of the man and bent down, wrapping his clawed hand around his throat and hoisting him up off the ground with ease. "You may call me, Legion!" He drained away the man's soul then, amid the shadows of a side street under flickering lights, and walked away as the sun dipped below the horizon.

A New Day

The man walked down the street as the sun came up, his beard tickling his chest. He had cast away the rosary—the pieces clattering down a sewer drain—and had taken off the white collar. It had been a long time since he had a beard, but he didn't dislike it. He tipped his wide brim hat to a passing woman on a bike and she waved at him in that coy way humans did. He walked into the diner as it opened its doors and settled down at a booth, taking the menu from the young waitress that seated him. The television rambled on in the background as the news broadcast droned on.

"What can I get you this morning?" she asked, taking out her little notepad.

"I'll have a cup of coffee. Black." The man kept his hands on his lap as the feeling of the sun on his face through the window warmed him slightly. It had been so long since he had a face that wasn't damaged.

"By the way, I love your eyes," the young waitress said. "I've never seen two eyes that were different colors before."

Nergal looked up at her and smiled. "What a coincidence," he replied sitting back. "Neither have I." He would've said more but the commotion at the counter drew his attention. The patrons were all pointing at the television and by the excited tones, it was bad news. *It is dawn in the glorious city of Miami and nothing can ruin my day,* Nergal regretted that thought as the next instant everything went to hell. The diner imploded and turned most everything in it to ash within seconds. Nergal's body, though mortal, housed an angelic essence-so it was a little more resilient than most. Still, he was thrown through the large window and down the street as flames burned away his clothes, face, and knickknacks. He screamed in anguish as he slammed into a truck that then exploded and burned the fallen angel even more. His last sight was of the entire horizon burning, when he finally faded into oblivion. *Well looks like I'm without a body once more...*

The Cure

THE PRIEST COMES

The priest walked slowly down the dark streets of the Virginia Council States, intent on his thoughts as the moon fought the clouds for dominance. He liked this place—more so than any of the other rebuilt city states—because they valued the tenets of democracy and had a council of nine that voted on most policies-not like that dictator in New Dallas. Here, the remnants of Virginia, West Virginia, and the tattered remains of Maryland came together and rebuilt, favoring hospitals over anything else. It made his heart soar that humanity could do something like that, though they still needed a lot of work.

The wind blew his coat around like a rag doll as he shook his head and went back to thoughts of his current dilemma-stopping that murderer. The priest was old, older than he should be, and he had known about this man for many years. Yet, Father had forbidden him to end the problem once and for all. Father Michael stopped at a corner as the stop sign bent in the wind; he looked both ways before stepping into the street. He didn't need to, but it was a habit he had grown accustomed to over the many years. At first glance he was nothing special to look at. He was of average height and weight, nearing six feet and handsome by modern standards, his black clothing hung comfortably on his frame, and his golden hair fell neatly to his shoulders. However, it was his eyes that most people remembered. His bright blue eyes seemed like pools of sky that could see into your very soul, and tell you what you hated about yourself the most.

Father Michael looked up as he walked, silently praying at the vanishing moon, and ignored the cars that were screeching to a halt and blaring their horns at the next intersection. *You know I could fix this once and for all...* he thought, finally acknowledging the drivers that were yelling obscenities at him, despite his white collar. *I know you forbade it, yet I can't help but say again that it would be for the best.* Hearing no response, as usual, he sighed and walked on. Faith was one of those things that humanity took for granted, yet even the most faithful had their doubts now and again. As he approached the hospital, his thoughts turned towards the helpless child he knew was suffering inside. The poor child was going to die soon, and there was nothing anyone could do. *So why is that murderer coming here?* he asked himself, as he walked up to the main doors.

"Evening, Father," the security guard greeted him, waving him on through the metal detector and nodding to the man at the door. "He's fine, Joe, I vouch for him."

Father Michael stopped in front of the man at the door, a new guard he hadn't met yet and saw the man's doubt. "It's all right, my child, you don't have to take his word," he said, holding up his arms and turning slowly so the man could check him once more. The youth in the Virginia Council States had become brazen with their attacks on the hospital pharmacy this past year and security had become worse here than at the airports. Still, as humanity rebuilt, this was one of the better places in the ruined world.

"Sorry, Father," Joe said, frisking him quickly and then bowing his head.

"Nothing to be sorry about," Michael replied, touching two fingers upon the man's brow and whispering a quick prayer. The man's eyes lit up and he breathed a sigh of relief. Father Michael left them behind, chuckling at their fading conversation. He got into the elevator and pressed the number four, watching the metal doors close, and hearing their wonder. He had that affect on people.

A Mother's Worry

She watched the restraints go taut as her son thrashed on the table despite the drugs coursing through his system. Frustrated tears made their way down her stoic face as she kept glancing at the monitor, praying for some sign of a change as the timer sped on. Nothing. It had been over thirty seconds and the treatment was doing absolutely nothing to abate the rage that was slowly eating her son alive.

Dr. Sandra Cain reached over and hit the call button with shaking hands. "All right, Fran, you can untie him," she said, releasing the button and sitting back with a heavy sigh. She blew a strand of dirty blond hair out of her deep brown eyes as her assistant walked towards the table. With a hesitation born of past mistakes, she cautiously untied the seven-year-old boy. Once the restraints were off, the boy calmed down immediately, sat up, and looked around with confusion in his eyes. It happened like this every time the rage came on. If restrained, it would grow worse-yet, left alone, the boy would turn violent within hours. Being restrained seemed to burn off the rage, but the damage it was doing to the small child's body wasn't good at all. Another year of this and it would start to shut down.

"Didn't we agree you weren't treating your own son anymore, Sandra?" a stern voice asked from the doorway behind her.

Sandra sat up and swore under her breath, berating herself for not hearing the door open. "Vincent, I just wanted to try the new serum I had been working on when you took over the case."

The man walked in and sat in the chair next to her, his dark hair falling into his face. Brushing it to the side, Dr. Vincent Wu set down his clipboard and leaned back, irritation clear on his visage. "You're too close to this one, Sandra. Please let me treat your son and I promise you we will find a way to get past his rage."

"It's killing him and you know it, Vincent."

"I know you think that, but there is very little evidence to support that this build up of anger is hurting him long term, other than your family research that is."

"We have had only three boys born into my family survive over the last two hundred years, and only one in the last fifty," Sandra started saying, standing and pacing around the room, her emotions getting the better of her calculating mind. "All the other boys that were born died within eight to ten years; that cannot be a coincidence."

Dr. Wu sat up a little straighter, smoothing out his white coat and swiveling around to face her directly. "It's either IED or ODD, Sandra. We've all agreed, except Dr. Harrison who says it's IED with Bipolar."

"He's an idiot."

"You're not wrong on that account, yet it holds more water than *your* theory," Vincent said, softening his voice. "Listen, I know you care...If he were my son...."

"But he's not," Sandra said with an air of finality. She turned to the glass and saw Aleksandr looking at her, fear in his uncertain eyes. Sandra smiled and raised her fingers to her eyes, her heart, and then back to him. *I love you.* He made the sign back and then followed the assistant out of the room, his head hung down.

"Go home for now and we'll look at his charts again in the morning and see what your serum did or didn't do. Don't worry, I said I would share everything we found and I still hold to that. Who knows, maybe the new serum did something after all," Vincent said, patting her on the arm as he stood. "Mercy General has the brightest minds in all of the Virginia Council States, Sandra, yours included."

"All right, I'll just say goodnight to Alek and then I'll go get some sleep," Sandra said, laying a hand on her colleague's shoulder. "Just keep a close eye on him through the night."

"We'll keep him monitored, don't worry," Vincent agreed as she walked towards the door.

Sandra left wondering if they would ever find out what was wrong with her baby boy.

The Stranger and the Rage

She walked out and went to her son's room to say good bye, but when she turned the corner she hit a wall of some kind and fell back. Landing on her backside, she looked up to see what she ran into and gasped. The man staring down at her was dressed in faded jeans and a tight white t-shirt. His jacket looked worn and very old, like it was his grandfathers, and his piercing eyes were the color of wet dirt; a deep brown that seemed made of the very earth itself. He had long brown hair and tanned skin on a massive frame filled with corded muscle. "I'm...I'm sorry I didn't see you there," she stammered as she tried to stand on wobbly legs.

The man smiled; a cold smile that didn't seem to touch his eyes. Like he had seen everything and didn't like any of it. "It's my fault, I wasn't even looking up," he said, helping her stand. "I was actually looking for you, Sandra."

"Do I know you?" she asked, knowing full well that if she had ever seen this man before she would've have remembered it-remembered it and dreamt about it for years. Being a single mom to a child that was this ill had left her social life dying in a ditch, yet she could still dream of it now and again.

"No. I'm a friend of your father. My name is Adam," the man said, walking with her as they talked. "I'm here because of your son."

Sandra stopped, an icy hand gripping her spine, all thoughts of flirting gone in a heartbeat. "What do you know about my son?"

"I know that he has a...rage that he can't control. I know," he went on, forestalling her with a raised finger, "that he is getting worse and that the doctors all think it's some sort of mental disorder. I think differently."

Sandra looked into Adam's eyes and saw sadness, like he knew exactly what she was feeling. "You've lost someone like this before haven't you?"

"Yes I have; I've only been able to save one so far. I'm hoping that your son will be the second, but there isn't much time." Adam turned the corner and stopped before her son's door. He cocked his head to one side and listened at the door, then nodded. "Coast is clear."

Sandra watched him open the door and walk in; going right to her son's bed even though there was another boy in the room. That icy hand twisted the spine it had grabbed and sent that chill straight into her gut. "Wait, how do you know about Denis again?" she asked, trying to trick him by giving him a false name.

Adam turned, smiling again and actually laughed. "*Aleksandr* has the same symptoms that the other boys had," he said walking over and patting the boy on the head lightly.

"Don't touch me!" the boy screamed, his eyes wide and his veins in his neck popping out. His adrenalin was flushing again, that fight or flight kicking in every time that the rage did. "Don't you hurt her!"

"Alek, it's all right," Adam said, placing his hand on the boy and closing his eyes. The boy closed his eyes as well and laid back down, breathing normally once more.

"How did you?"

"Listen, were almost out of time, Michael will be here any minute."

"Father Michael? How do you know him?" Sandra's head was spinning.

"Father? He is no priest, but that doesn't matter. All that matters is that you take this and make a serum out of it," Adam said, handing her a vial full of what looked like blood.

"What is this?" Sandra asked as she took the dark vial, her thoughts whirling quickly as she took it all in. *If Father Michael isn't a priest, then what is he?* Father Michael had taken to visiting the boy off and on since she had admitted him last year. The man seemed fine enough, if a little eccentric at times.

"It's a vial of my blood. Trust me, I'm a match for your son and that will be able to cure him of what has gripped him."

"How are you...*Who* are you?" Sandra asked, the room now spinning to match her head. "You said you knew my father," Sandra said, a tone of distrust clear in her voice.

"I did know Frank; very well in fact." Adam turned to face her, his smile somehow genuine this time. "He always talked about his little whelp Sandra and how she always knew best," Adam said softly as if he were remembering her father fondly. "I'm...family. That's all you need to know."

Sandra nodded dumbly, all distrust gone with those haunting words. Her father did indeed used to call her that, and no one could've known except a good friend; her father never confided in *anyone*. The man was too stubborn.

Adam walked around her and went to the door, listening again. "Now, I want you to lock this behind me and do *not* come out no matter what you hear," Adam told her as he opened it, looking back one last time. "Just please make that serum tonight and everything else will be fine." Once she nodded, Adam left and closed the door.

The Meeting of the Two

Father Michael got off the elevator and saw him, standing there in the hallway just like any normal human being; but the large man was anything but normal. "There you are," Father Michael said, squaring his shoulders and letting his coat fall to the floor. "I've been looking for you, Cain."

"I go by Adam these days, Michael."

"Adam? Is that some sort of sick joke? You are a murderer. Why would you take the name of your father and soil it like that?"

"You wouldn't understand family, Michael; you angels have no souls, so the concept doesn't mean anything to you."

"I understand that the boy in there can't be allowed to live with the curse you passed on to him." Michael walked forward, flexing his shoulders and letting his wings come out; the bright white feathers brushed the walls on either side of the hallway. All angels had wings that no one could see. They were kept discorporate behind them, almost inside of them. When released, humanity could no longer perceive the angel unless that angel wished them to. Thankfully, Cain could see his wings regardless because of the curse laid on him by God. Michael didn't have to worry about any bystanders seeing his wings if they happened by.

"He *will* live, Michael, just like David did two hundred years ago," the man called Cain said as he spread his feet apart, balancing on the balls of his feet. "And those wings won't help you this time."

"How are you going to save this child when you couldn't save the others?" Michael asked, his sword manifesting in his right hand by sheer will alone. He couldn't kill Cain permanently, but he could take him out for awhile while the cursed man healed. The archangel had done this over and over through the years—ever since most of the angels came down after humanity broke the world— always putting the man down when he could find him. Cain couldn't truly die, but he took a long time to come back depending on how bad he was.

"I gave the mother a vial of my blood."

"You what!?" Michael yelled, caught completely off guard for the first time in centuries. The implications were staggering. Maybe now Father would allow him to slay all the progeny of Cain and be done with it. "They can't learn of divinity, Cain!"

"And they won't. Don't you see Michael? The humans today don't want to believe," Cain said, walking slowly towards the angel with his hands out wide. "Remember that video of me falling off the building in New Seattle last year? It went viral and everyone thought it was photo shopped."

"But..."

"And that video of Gabriel in the Russian Faction States, saving that kid on a bike. They labeled it part of a video game!" Cain stopped a mere two feet away from the archangel, still smiling. "They really don't want to see what is right in front of them."

Michael closed his eyes, hating what the man was saying but finding no argument. He struck quickly, plunging his sword towards Cain's chest. The move was so fast that any normal being would be impaled, yet Cain had been killing since the first days of humanity and it was hard to catch him off guard.

Cain twisted and slapped the sword out wide, the flames on the divine relic burning his flesh. He punched Michael once, twice, and a third time in the face, staggering the archangel despite the divine power in him.

Michael smiled as his superficial wounds were already healing and then spun, using his wings to slam the big man against the wall. The archangel spun once more, kicking Cain in the chest and then thrusting the sword again, this time piercing him in the center of his chest, the flaming sword searing the flesh and biting into bone.

Cain gritted his teeth through the pain and tried to push back, yet his great strength was already failing.

Michael yanked the sword free, feeling blood splatter his face as Cain spit his defiance to the mortal wound. Michael ignored the insult and grabbed Cain's jacket, holding him up. "Seems that the wings did help me after all, right Cain?" Michael asked as the light dimmed in the cursed man's eyes. The archangel spun towards the windows, flying out in a spray of blood and glass. He dropped the body over the river and soared up into the clouds. He was going to go and stop the mother, yet Cain's words stalled his hand. *They better not find out about us, Cain...*

The Cure

Sandra opened the door quietly after five minutes of silence went by. She had heard fighting and glass breaking, yet she held her promise to keep the door locked. She crept into the hallway and stopped as she took in the blood splattered walls and broken windows. There was no sign of either Adam or Father Michael. As the elevator dinged and security men poured out with their walkie-talkies, Sandra snuck down to the lab and started work on the blood she had been given. It was well after hours and no one would even notice that she was here until it was too late. After a couple minutes of getting things ready, she took the specimen and loaded some onto the glass under the microscope. She was astounded at what she was seeing.

Science had reached the point where they could tell a person's biological age by analyzing proteins in the blood. By measuring the levels of an enzyme, called alkaline phosphates, they could track the changes in the body between childhood and adulthood. The levels in the blood before her had to be wrong. She checked it twice, then rubbed her eyes once more. It said that the age of the body was at least four millennia old, if not more. *I'll think about that another day*, Sandra thought as she got to work.

It took her well into the morning to come up with a workable serum—one that wasn't even tested—but she somehow believed the man. No one bothered her work, well past hours in the hospital, mainly because of the police investigating the blood and broken four-story windows. Walking toward her son's room with the syringe in her pocket, she looked up to the ceiling and silently prayed. *God, let this work...I just want my son to live*, she thought as she neared her son's new room. Her stomach dropped as she saw it was empty.

"Oh, Miss Cain, we moved your son down one floor to the cancer wing as the police are still working on this floor," one of the night nurses said coming down the hall. "Room 335."

Sandra nodded and walked quickly to the elevator, hitting the button with rising anxiety. She almost jogged to her son's new room. She opened the door to the room and froze as she saw someone sitting in the chair in the corner.

"Hello, Sandra. Pray, come in and shut the door."

"Who are you?" Sandra asked, backing up a little, ready to fight for her son. She could see Aleksandr tossing fitfully in his sleep, the veins in his neck pulsing softly. It was getting worse.

"My name is Gabriel and let's just say that I'm here to make sure this gets done without interference," the man said, standing up and brushing off his white suit. He had long dirty blond hair and green eyes like liquid emeralds.

"Are you a friend of Father Michael?" Sandra asked, remembering what Adam had said about the man not being a priest. Yet there was something calming about this man standing before her and she found herself relaxed despite the fear of her son's condition.

"Michael and I don't always see eye to eye, but yes, I know him. Please, give your son the shot and let's pray together," Gabriel said, waving her over to her son's side as he stepped away.

Aleksandr was almost panting now, close to either a seizure or waking up in a fit of rage like he had been doing for months. She had to hurry before the monitors showed his signs and alarms went off. Sandra wiped his arm with the sterile wipe in her pocket and gave him the shot, closing her eyes and clutching the boy's arm. Minutes dragged on like years as the boy fought for control.

"Hey, it will be all right," Gabriel said, moving impossibly fast to stand by the woman's side as she started to lean. He knew that she was at the human limit for endurance with all of this.

"How do you know that?" Sandra asked, yawning yet never letting her son go.

Gabriel smiled, remembering what his sister had said about this human. "Well, I have it on the *highest* authority that your son will be fine. After all, family is the most important thing in this life," Gabriel said, but she was already fading, her eyes closing despite her reluctance.

The archangel guided her to the chair in the corner, then went to check on the boy. Sure enough, his breathing was slowing down and the veins were easing up. The rage, brought on from the Mark of Cain—passed down to all males of his line—was being brought to heel. Gabriel lifted the boy's sleeve and saw the birthmark, a plain circle upon his bicep, start to fade. It was rare to bear a son from the blood of Cain, but not impossible. They all died from the curse God had laid upon the first murderer; yet, He was not all condemning. This one would live and go on to do great things, but Gabriel's job wasn't done. He still had to find Michael and have the 'talk' he was dreading. But that was a problem for another day.

Threads of Fate

Timing

The man walked into the bar, greeted by a sudden, uneasy, silence. He looked around the local dive and grinned, brushing his slick blond hair back out of his brilliant hazel eyes. He was dressed in an Armani suit, complete with silver cuff links and polished shoes; he fit in with the crowd like a construction worker at a baby shower. After a few seconds of awkward quiet, the patrons started talking once more and the man sauntered over to the bar, stepping over a body on the floor.

"Bourbon, neat," the man told the bartender, leaning on the bar with an ease that spoke volumes as he watched the crowd. He wasn't afraid of anything or anyone here and it showed clearly in his posture.

"I think you're in the wrong place, mister," The bartender said as he poured the man's drink.

The man turned, his stare intense, and the bartender fell back a step. "I'm looking for a couple of guys that work for the local art gallery," he said, his penetrating gaze holding the human before him. Not many could look him in the eye and hold that gaze. It was said that you could see your own soul in his eyes.

"They're over there," the man answered, backing away. "Who *are* you?"

The man flipped him a coin, ignoring the question with practiced ease. "Here, for your troubles." The coin landed on the bar and spun, never slowing down.

The bartender grabbed it and yelled, dropping the coin. "Why is it *hot*?" the bartender asked, his voice rising in fear.

The man ignored the question, knowing that in a few minutes the bartender would pick it up anyway. Greed was his favorite sin, and it was so easy to use against these people. He walked over to the table and pulled out a chair, never bothering to ask if he could sit.

"Good evening, gentleman. My name is Natasha," the man lied, sitting down as they all stood up. "Oh, please," he started, dropping a wad of cash on the table as if it were a ball of lint taking up too much room in his pocket. As expected, they all sat down, staring at the money in front of him. "That's better. I have a job for you and it pays very well." The man, who was using the name Natasha for now, explained the plan in detail to them, his words making sense even though they would probably be caught. He had a way with words after all. *And if things go right, then all my plans will start to come together. A hint here, a warning there, and the children will someday meet,* he thought as he stood and left the bar, whistling a merry tune. *And when that happens, well, we will see what else can spring up.*

Arrival

Aleksandr Devir rode his Harley down Roanoke Way as the strong gusts blew off of lake Washington. The lingering sunset lent a touch of eerie spectacle to the surrounding landscape and the winds swept his long, raven hair back like a flag in a hurricane. He wasn't in a hurry; being immortal did have its advantages after all. His god given name was Azrael; he spent his time helping souls that were reluctant to go to heaven. These souls were—more often than not—in almost complete balance, neither good nor evil in life. He was often called the Angel of Death, a title that really got misconstrued through the centuries. He was one of the seven archangels of heaven and had been here on earth for millennia, unlike some of his brothers and sisters that came down when the humans broke the world. He had come to the city of New Seattle because of a vision of this particular home here on Mercer Island Retreat; someone was going to die and be in balance. He didn't always get these visions, but when he did, they were always important.

New Seattle had been very lucky during the calamity, as most everything west of the city went under when California was lost. They had survived and built a massive seawall, sheltering the city and surrounding Mercer Island Retreat, which now served as the home of the wealthy and powerful. Pulling over at the house, he shut off the bike and set the kickstand. He looked around the street and let out a whistle. It was a *very* nice neighborhood, but then again, he had seen them all over the years. *People with money have always known how to flaunt it,* Aleksandr thought, getting off the bike. Dressed in ripped jeans, t-shirt, and a leather jacket—not unheard of in New Seattle—he was completely out of place in this neighborhood.

"Hi there," a small voice said from behind him.

Aleksandr turned, his ice blue eyes searching for the origin of the voice, and settled on a small child. The boy had to be at least seven years old and his innocence radiated out from him like a furnace. "Hello to you as well, little one."

"My mommy says you're not supposed to ride without a helmet," the young one admonished, fists on his hips. He had dark skin, very short hair, and eyes like pools of liquid chocolate.

"Well, she would be right. In fact my father would be displeased as well," Aleksandr said, laughing at the little one's stance. This didn't seem like the sort of place for a person to die in balance. *Maybe the vision was for someone else?* Aleksandr asked himself.

"You look like you need a good meal," the boy said, walking up and grabbing the archangel's hand, leading him towards the house. "My mom makes the best food. You'll love it."

"I'm not sure this is a good idea, little one."

"Simon."

"What now?"

"My name is Simon. What's yours?" the young boy asked. He had a complete lack of fear and it was both unnerving and refreshing at the same time; in this world now-a-days, you just didn't see it.

"Oh. My name is Aleksandr." He looked up as he was pulled along, seeing the mother standing at the open door watching them. Not that the boy could've pulled him; hell, five men couldn't pull him if he didn't want them to.

"Now who is this, Simon?" the woman asked, not irritated, nor angry in the slightest. "I swear you find the strangest pets."

"I'm sorry ma'am. He is a spirited little one." Aleksandr was in a difficult situation. He usually never made contact with the people he interacted with, often using his wings as cover. Angels could walk among the humans, but once their wings came out, it was like the angel disappeared. If they really wanted to show themselves, they had to will it, but that only happened rarely, as their father didn't approve of it. Still, Aleksandr had his moments when he dallied in the affairs of mortals and he wanted to show them, but this was not that day.

"Oh, it's fine," the woman said, a broad smile upon her face. "He does this from time to time, we're used to it." She had long black hair and dark eyes, her yellow sun dress a bright contrast to her marble smooth dark skin.

Nodding, Aleksandr went into the house, worried about what would happen this night that would've called him here.

THE HOST

Aleksandr stood in what could only be called a mansion. Whatever this family did for work was clearly one of the higher paying jobs in this new world, yet they didn't over do it. Oh sure, there were expensive paintings and such, but the place really was humble. It was the things that only *he* could see that told the true story. The father, dressed in a pair of slacks and a button up shirt, was standing near the bottom of the stairs under a cross that, to the archangel's eyes, was from the holy land itself. Made of Bethlehem wood, the cross radiated power to those that could sense it. There were other things, treasures really, that would seem ordinary to most people. What drew his gaze was the book in a glass case, written in the old tongue. He recognized it as one of the first bibles ever bound.

"You must be my son's new friend," the man said as he walked over. "My name is David Rand, and this is my wife, Mary. You've already met Simon." David shook Aleksandr's hand firmly, his warm, blue eyes assuring the archangel that he was welcome—a rare sight indeed, dressed as he was.

"My name is Aleksandr Devir. So nice to meet you all."

"You will join us as our guest, won't you?" David asked tilting his head and smirking.

"If it is not too much trouble," Aleksandr said, taking off his jacket. "Yet, if I may ask, why would you let your son drag a stranger into your house on a whim like this, Mr. Rand? I could be anyone."

"Well, I have learned to do unto others like you would have them do unto you. If I were lost and hungry, I would want someone to shelter and feed me."

"You're assuming I'm lost."

"Fair, but you didn't say you weren't hungry."

"All right, you have me there. Seriously though, in this age, you would take the chance I'm not here to rob you or worse?" He hated to bring it up, but it seemed so out of place with the world he was now walking. Fear and prejudice were commonplace, and no one did anything unless it was for themselves. It was even worse than that in the old cities and ruins.

"In all seriousness, Aleksandr, I do it *because* of this day and age." David turned and walked over to the book in the glass case, touching the glass reverently. "You see, someone has to make that step to show others that it's all right. That it's good to help someone in need. I have a lot of money and now I share it when I can."

"Is that why you collect holy relics?" Aleksandr asked, gaining a new respect for this human.

"You noticed those? Yes. I'm an art dealer-but when these came in, they weren't authenticated, so I bought them for my personal collection."

"So, you have an eye for things like this?" the archangel asked, getting that feeling in his spine that something else was going on here. *What have you dropped me into, Father?*

Mary's voice interrupted their conversation momentarily. "Dinner's ready!"

David walked by Aleksandr, placing his hand on the man's broad shoulder. "Not me. It's Simon that has the eye for these things."

Dinner Guest

Aleksandr followed David in silence. The boy had the Sight. *Could he see that I was an angel?* His thoughts spun as he pulled a chair out next to the child. *Was that why the boy wanted me to come in?*

"Do you want to say grace, Simon?" Mary asked as she brought in the last dish and set it down on the table.

Aleksandr saw the boy look at him instead and smiled. "Allow me," the archangel said, standing and bowing his head in reverence. "Oh Father, bless this family for reaching out to a stranger and inviting him into their loving home. Bless this food that we break in your name and feast on because of your benevolence. In your name we pray, Amen."

"Well said, man," David replied with an enthusiasm that seemed out of place. "Too long this house has gone without a proper grace." The man ran his hand over his bald head as he laughed and winked at Simon.

"Now dear, let's not start that again," Mary said, her tone agitated. She turned to Aleksandr and sighed. "Ever since Simon almost died and David found God, he's been somewhat of a preacher in the household. Don't get me wrong, I go to church and believe in God and all, but..."

"But sometimes that's enough, right?" Aleksandr asked, echoing the all too real viewpoint of most of the angels. He knew that was all his Father ever wanted, but it always got blown out of proportion by the churches; it had since the beginning. "He works in mysterious ways though, and if your son was spared, then it was for a reason." Aleksandr leaned back and looked over at Simon, then back to David. "If I may ask...what happened to him?"

David looked down at his hands as he wrung them together in guilt. "It was an accident at one of our sites. We were in Old California Island saving relics from a half sunken church when a crate fell off of a fork lift; I was only trying to show Simon where I work. We flew him home as fast as we could, but the doctors said he wouldn't regain consciousness from the coma. The very next day he was awake and asking for us, though; it was a miracle."

"Well, you really are blessed, aren't you Simon?" Aleksandr rubbed the boys head, eliciting a smile.

"Amen to that," David said as he grabbed a platter. "Aleksandr, try Mary's ham." He was desperately trying to change the subject, which was weird for someone supposedly into religion. Most people that 'found' God tended to babble endlessly about their new views.

Aleksandr took the platter and took a helping for himself. He turned to Simon to offer some and saw the boy staring back at the glass case. He leaned down and whispered into the boy's ear. "You can see it glow, can't you?" the archangel asked, guessing that the boy could see the divinity in certain objects. Often people like this developed the sense after a near death experience, but most ignored it—unless they were fully exposed to something they couldn't un-see. Aleksandr turned again to the table before the parents caught on to their whispered conversation. *I must be here for the boy,* he thought as he broke his fast with these kind souls. *He must be in balance because of guilt.*

Though rare, it was not unheard of to feel such guilt that it stained your very soul with the taint of evil. Such people often condemned themselves, thinking they deserved it as a form of punishment. These souls stayed here on earth after death, wandering as lost spirits—or ghosts as humanity liked to call them—forever lamenting their sins until their guilt or other unresolved issues were addressed and they could make their way to heaven. The irony that the very world they lived in was their version of Hell was lost on them all. In this case, the boy was pure so his guilt shifted him into balance, though that was purely conjecture.

"So. what brings you to New Seattle?" David asked the archangel

"My Father said I would find something important here."

"And did you? Find something that is?"

" So far, I think I did. I just have to wait and see," Aleksandr said trying to skirt the subject. "So, David, what did you do before you started collecting religious art?" Before the man could answer, the sound of splintering wood and shouts echoed from the foyer as men crashed in waving firearms.

Revelations

Aleksandr saw the uninvited guests fire two rounds into the ceiling to make their point, and it worked rather well for the Rand family. Mary grabbed Simon and slipped under the table, while David came around with his hands in the air.

"Please...take whatever you want, just don't hurt us," he begged as the men came into the dining room.

"Who do we have here?" one of the thugs asked, looking at Aleksandr. He leveled the gun at the archangel's face and cocked his head to one side. "Don't scare easily do you, big man?"

"Well, you would have to be a threat for me to be scared," Aleksandr countered easily, a smile on his face. He flexed his shoulders as he crossed his powerful arms, He was fairly certain that he could scare these brutes off without a scene, yet sadly, the courage of a small boy thwarted that.

"You leave my friend alone!" Simon screamed, breaking away from his mother's grasp. He ran for

Aleksandr, putting himself in front of the archangel; for a split second, time slowed to a halt.

Aleksandr saw the thug reflexively aim the gun at Simon, and pull the trigger, firing at what had drawn his attention. Aleksandr had less than a second to save the boy, yet David beat the angel of death to it.

The man leapt into the path of the bullet, taking the shot meant for his own son. In that perfect moment the father had made the only choice left to him-to save his child. Aleksandr unfurled his great raven black wings, willing them *all* to see, Dad be damned. He was Azrael now and these thugs would pay. The men all stopped, some of them crying out and falling to prostrate themselves, and Azrael used that distraction to move among them with unbridled fury. His fists connected, breaking bones and sending the men flying; he was strong, stronger than anything they had ever encountered and within seconds it was over. The wailing of Mary brought the archangel back to reality.

"David please...David no!"

Wings put away once more, Aleksandr went to the downed man and saw that the bullet had hit his right arm; not fatal by any means, yet David was deathly pale and sweating. The man was having a heart attack.

"Hang on David..." Aleksandr started to say, but stopped when he saw the soul start to peel away and float out of the body, turning this way and that as if lost. David's eyes fluttered and closed, as his last breath escaped his body. *Oh Father,* he thought, *I'm not here for the boy...I'm here for him!* The archangel walked over and gently took hold of the soul, sending reassuring thoughts to it.

"Can he still hear me?" Simon asked in a small voice, his tears dropping from his face like rain.

"You can see him?"

"Yes. Can I say good bye?"

"You most certainly can, though he can't answer you back." The archangel looked at Mary and saw that she was in such shock that none of this was registering. That in itself was a blessing.

"Goodbye, father, I will look after mom. Try not to worry, I'll make you proud!" Simon finished and broke down into sobs as he stumbled over to his mother and hugged her.

Aleksandr, or Azrael as he was known, lifted the soul of David Rand up high and willed him towards the light. The man must've done some questionable things before finding his faith, but that one selfless act had brought him into balance. *Go in peace David, you saved your son.*

Answers

Aleksandr grabbed his jacket and left the house quickly as sirens wailed in the distance. He knew that the mother and son needed to be alone right now, and that his time among them was over. Still, he would always remember these people fondly. He had been down here among humanity for eons and had grown to love these fragile beings, maybe even more than Father did. The hair on the back of his neck rising brought him out of his thoughts. Aleksandr sensed his brother in the darkness before he actually saw him; the devil was leaning on his Harley, slowly clapping his hands with a broad smile upon his angelic face.

"My my, you took your wings out and everything, Azrael? Color me impressed," the man going by Natasha said.

"This was your doing wasn't it, Lucifer?" Aleksandr stormed towards his fallen brother, storm clouds gathering on his brow.

"Yes, it was, dear brother, but you know I only do things for the right reasons," the fallen archangel replied as he stood, bracing for anything.

" So you always say, yet what did this accomplish then?" Aleksandr asked, his ire rising towards his lost brother. He tried to clamp down on his anger, knowing that it would do no good anyway.

"Those men would've stormed this house three days from now and killed everyone inside. They worked for Rand Incorporated and knew that David had procured some priceless relics. Their greed would drive them to finally act on their impulses and rashly at that. Young Simon would never go on to greatness and instead, pass on to heaven." Lucifer turned as the police car screeched around the corner and unfolded his white majestic wings.

"So, you had them come early knowing I would be here?" Aleksandr asked, his wings coming out once more to keep these officers from seeing him as well. He understood the motive, yet hated the fact that a good man had died.

"Yes. I turned them into a surgical knife instead of an axe. I knew you would protect the child and I assumed David would die in the crossfire. Imagine my surprise when it was his heart that did it."

"Well, you got your wish, Lucifer. The child can *see* and will probably learn all sorts of things from those relics in there," Aleksandr shouldered past his brother and got on his bike, driving off without a second glance at his brother.

Lucifer watched his brother fold in his black wings and drive off around the corner. *First, I tipped off Gabriel about Cain and Michael, now I've saved a Seer,* he thought as he beat his wings, ascending into the sky. *All my plans are coming together.* The fallen archangel flew up into the clouds, heading to his next appointment with fate. It came in handy that he could glimpse the near future, and he would save them all...even if it killed him.

Seeing the Light

To Forget

The morning light washed over her, warming skin that was exposed to the gentle spring breeze. The woman didn't seem to notice the beautiful dawn coming over the great sea wall as she stood on the precipice of the tall building, head skyward and eyes closed, gentle tears gliding down her cheeks. The woman never even heard the horns and general bustle of the traffic below, the New Seattle morning commute well underway. Dressed in a diaphanous yellow nightgown, Amanda Slone only had one thought on this bright sunny Thursday; she was going to end it all.

She had been through so much these last six months; the pain of loss and suffering too hard to bear anymore. Her life was in shambles since her twin brother had died—debt piling up and her job gone because she couldn't focus anymore. Since that fateful day, she had been walking around in a kind of daze, her mind numb to the whole world around her. Her friends had tried to get her to move on, even setting her up a couple times, but she just couldn't feel anything anymore except the void inside her chest. She just wanted it all over and to forget this life.

It's for the better, she thought as the wind shifted

and blew her strawberry-blond hair into her deep green eyes. Her hair pushed the tears across her face as she leaned forward just a little. *No one will miss me anyway.*

"View is pretty good from up here, isn't it?" a voice asked from right behind her.

Amanda screamed; her tranquility was shattered as she pitched forward off the ledge with flailing arms. A strong hand wrapped around her waist, holding her as she looked down the four stories to the streets of downtown New Seattle. Still screaming, Amanda was hauled back in and let go. She spun around, her instincts crying for flight, yet she was held by the curiosity that plagued all of humankind. There in front of her stood a man dressed in ripped jeans, a white t-shirt, and a leather jacket. He had long raven black hair and ice blue eyes that seemed to see through her. Amanda wrapped her arms around herself as she looked at him, feeling naked under that gaze in more ways than one, the breeze cutting right through her nightgown. "Who...who are you?"

The man took off his jacket, his smile washing over her as surely as the light from the rising sun. "My name is Aleksandr," the man said, wrapping his jacket around her shoulders as she flinched. "It's alright, I won't hurt you." Aleksandr backed up and bowed slightly, giving her space.

Amanda looked around in a daze, her thoughts muddled and scattered like leaves caught in a wind gust. She would've been dead by now if it weren't for this man and she wasn't sure if that angered her or not. "What are you doing up here?" she asked as she looked around nervously. She was sure she had wedged the door shut so that this wouldn't happen. Amanda glanced at the door to the building and did indeed see that the metal bar she had placed was still secure. Backing away from him slowly, she tried to think of how else he could've gained access to the roof, but her brain was numb. *Oh God, if only I could stop feeling like this.*

"I saw you there on the ledge and was pretty sure you were going to do something you might regret, so I came to talk." Aleksandr held his hands out wide and eased away trying to make her feel better. "I'm sorry if I'm worrying you."

Amanda scanned the roof around them and stopped cold as she noticed the man's shadow. It was warped somehow, showing something like wings behind him as the sun rose on the horizon, but there was nothing there; they just didn't match. "Why does your shadow..." she started but froze as he chuckled.

"You know, I think I can help you with that fuzzy feeling," Aleksandr said as his voice changed subtly. He reached out impossibly fast and touched two fingers to her head, whispering something under his breath.

Amanda's mind seemed to snap into place, like it had been trying to squeeze into a dress one size too small and someone undid the zipper. The constant numb feeling was gone and her head was clear and rational for the first time in months. Amanda backed up warily, yet she couldn't help but smile at the feeling coming over her; she suddenly felt like she knew him—had always known him.

CLEAR HEAD

"Feeling better now?" Aleksandr pulled out an old flip phone from his back pocket and typed something in, then closed it again and put it away. The man went on like he didn't just perform a slight miracle, or had a deformed shadow. "So, my brother wants to meet with me in an hour, but I can spare some time for a cup of coffee," Aleksandr said, holding out his hand. "Wanna get dressed and grab one with me?"

Amanda knew Aleksandr was trying to change the subject, hoping she would just forget what she saw, or what he did. "Just how did you notice me on the ledge again?" She circled him slowly, staring at the shadow as she did. "The roof door is still locked and there isn't another way up here that I know of."

Aleksandr sighed, his broad shoulders slumping as if his secret had been discovered. "I see that you're one of those bright souls that catch more than most." He moved around her and closed his eyes, flexing his arms out wide. Huge raven, black wings spread out behind him, the feathers filtering the rays of sunlight from the sky. He stood there, majestic and terrible with a smile that told anyone looking that everything would be all right.

"You're...you..." Amanda went to church everyday growing up and knew her bible stories, yet it couldn't be.

"Yes, Amanda, I'm an angel," Aleksandr said. "I'm actually an archangel, to be precise."

"I never told you my name."

"You didn't need to, I know who you are," the archangel said, rising into the air slightly as he flapped his wings slowly. "I've been watching you ever since Greg died."

A tingle went down her spine at the mention of her brother. Greg had died in a car crash six months ago, torn from her soul and leaving her with a hole in herself she couldn't fill. The grief came washing back, yet it was different somehow. Amanda fought back tears and tried to get more out of the strange angelic being. "So, you're the archangel Alek? That doesn't ring any bells from Sunday school."

Aleksandr laughed at that and set down on the rooftop once more. "No, my name is actually Azrael, but most people don't react well to that name. My brothers can get away with using their own names, Michael and Gabriel are common enough, but some of us have to go by aliases."

Amanda shivered and it had nothing to do with the spring breeze or the translucent nightgown she was still wearing. The leather jacket he had draped around her shoulders slid off as she stood up straight. "You're *the* Azrael? The Angel of Death with the black cloak and the scythe from all those stories?" She backed away again, her fear rising. Had he killed Greg? Was he now here for her? *Oh God, what have I gotten myself into?*

"I dropped the scythe a long time ago and you didn't get yourself into anything Amanda, and yes I can hear prayers."

"I didn't pray for anything."

"You said my father's name and asked him something. I can hear those if I concentrate enough." Aleksandr folded his arms and leaned against a chimney, putting his wings away as easily as one might throw on a jacket. "My name has been misconstrued over the centuries, but yes, they call me the Angel of Death."

"Why have you been watching me then?"

"Because I deal in deaths that happen out of sequence and your life drew me in. You see, Greg was meant to pass that day, but you were meant to be there with him. Because you weren't, you were sent down a path you weren't supposed to be on." The Angel of Death walked towards her, his smile disarming. "Amanda, you aren't meant to die yet."

"Why would God take him like that?" Amanda was

crying again, dropping to her knees as the sadness flooded her, yet it felt different, like something was holding some of it back. "And why was I meant to be there? What would that have done?"

"You would've had this," Aleksandr said pulling something down from the sky. "Here, I'll make it so you can see him."

Amanda's eyes went wide as she saw her twin standing beside the archangel, his form almost see-through and insubstantial. His mouth moved, but she couldn't hear anything. Before she could ask, Greg rushed her and slammed into her, passing though her and leaving her sweating. "What just happened?"

"Now your soul is complete once more. Greg merged his soul with yours so that when you die, you both can ascend into heaven and not feel empty," Aleksandr replied softly, laying a hand on her shoulder. "Twins often do this to help the other when they pass, but you have to be close when they die."

Amanda was in awe, yet the pain was still there—pain and loss. "Why does it hurt so much?" she cried out, her face tilted towards the sky.

"That is because feeling the pain of loss is the price of a soul, Amanda. You all have the one thing angels don't, and with it comes a price, yet it's not all bad." He lifted her up, warmth spreading out from his hands and into hers. "My father also gave you such resilience that it astounds me to this day."

"But I almost—"

"I know, sometimes you humans just need a little boost. Answering a prayer here, leaving a despondent soul a sign there. That's why my brothers and sisters came down after the world broke, walking among you and trying to help. I've always been here, but that's another story for a different day."

"But surely priests can tell..."

"We remain unobserved, except to special cases like you, that can discern who or what we are."

"How am I special?" Things were coming at her so fast, she was confused; confused but not numb anymore. Her head was clear.

"That much is beyond even me, maybe Lucifer could tell, but he doesn't play well with others."

"The devil is real?"

"Yeah, well, he's not that bad, just a pain in the wings now and again." Aleksandr held out his hand once more. "Now, how about we go get that coffee? I'm sure Gabriel can wait a few more minutes."

Amanda reached out, a feeling of sureness coming over her. She took Aleksandr's hand and he picked up his jacket and pulled her into his arms, his wings coming out once more. "Things are going to be alright, now, aren't they?" she asked, her sadness still there, yet not overpowering. It was receding quickly now, and she liked to think Greg had that effect when he passed into her.

"In time they should be, yes. For now, let's just have some coffee and talk about your life and see what the positive things are and we can go from there. I know some great councilors you can see if you need it."

"Councilors?" Amanda asked "Like talking to an archangel isn't enough?"

Aleksandr laughed as he flew her down to her apartment patio, landing softly and opening her sliding door. "Trust me we're not experts. Now as much as I enjoy seeing you in that nightgown," he remarked with a wicked grin, "go get dressed and let's go. The rest of your life is waiting for you."

"You better be here when I get back." Amanda said, pointing a stern finger at him as she tried to hide her blush. *Did the Angel of Death just hit on me?* Her thoughts spun as she walked away and tried not to think of how gorgeous he looked.

"Don't worry Amanda, I'll be here. You would be surprised at how close we've been all along."

For the first time in six months, she felt alive. She was also wondering how much he had watched her while she was living in her nightmare of grief. She turned and went to get dressed, knowing that everything would be alright...she just had to have faith.

A Fresh Start

GRIEVANCES

He stomped away from the gun store, fuming over being rejected once more. He needed to protect himself from these...creatures, and no one would believe his stories. Darian Becket ignored the broken traffic lights and walked right into the street, horns blaring and tires screeching to a halt as the patched-together cars and trucks tried to avoid hitting him. He looked up through the black hair hanging in his grey eyes. "None of you get it do you?!" he yelled, his hysteria finally overwhelming him. He couldn't get a gun—he had tried three times here in Old Miami over the last month and if you couldn't get one here, then there wasn't anyone that would sell you one. Other weapons would probably be useless against these beings. The ruined city might be lawless, but the warlords controlled the guns like bankers did money.

Old Miami was a rarity, as most of the surrounding cities were flooded when the world broke. Here, at the tip of the state, the water had receded and the survivors had scrambled to erect some kind of wall to keep the sea water from submerging them completely during high tides. It had worked, somehow, but now the Warlords controlled everything.

Turning a corner and narrowly missing one of the city states enforcers on a motor bike, Darian's thoughts were singly focused on his problem. *What else could hurt an angel?* he asked himself as he walked on, bumping into more people carelessly as he fumed. Angels. He would have never even thought of such a thing unless he had seen proof with his own eyes.

It was three months ago, when his mother lost her job and his father had left them, that she had started praying again. His father was against it, but with him out of the picture, she jumped right back into it with fervor. Darian remembered scoffing at the idea, always laughing at her behind her back. That memory brought angry tears once more; the hate for these creatures building in him with every step. Angela Becket prayed for answers, for a sign, and it wasn't long after, that *he* came.

The man had introduced himself as Gabriel, a messenger from the church. He wore a white suit, immaculately clean, and carried a small white briefcase. He had long dirty blond hair and green eyes like liquid emeralds that could see into your very soul. Darian would never forget those eyes as long as he lived. The man came right to the door, knocking lightly, and walking right in as if he owned the place. Within minutes the man had his mother eating out of the palm of his hand, saying things like "It's what He wants," "It's His message," and "Just have faith."

Darian was suspicious and, of course, followed them around the house, listening to this man sweet talk his mother into whatever scheme he had going. Darian wasn't stupid, he knew the streets and how these guys operated. As they walked through the kitchen, heading for the living room, he saw the shadow of the man from the fading light of the setting sun through the window. The shadow was warped, showing wings on the man, even though there weren't any there. Frightened, he grabbed a large knife out of a wooden block near the stove, yelling for his mother to get away from the man. Darian remembered the man turning, a smile on his face as he looked down at his shadow, shaking his head sadly.

"I'm sorry son, not many people catch that," the man had said, a strange look in those emerald eyes.

Darian had panicked, adrenalin flooding his body, as the man took a step closer. He lunged with the knife, a killing blow with the force he put behind it; yet it never struck this being. His mother rushed in front of the man, yelling for Darian to stop. The knife plunged into her heart, his momentum carrying them both into the man; it was like hitting a wall. Gabriel caught them both effortlessly, and lowered them down. Angela Becket was dead before she hit the floor.

Darian stopped near an alley, the memory of his mother's death weighing on him. He looked and saw a man standing in the shadows, at ease, like he belonged there.

"What do *you* want, man?" Darian asked, stepping into the alley with a caution born of someone on the run. The stranger didn't seem like one of the warlords' enforcers, nor did he look like a drug runner.

"My name is Natasha and I want to help you with your...problem," the man said, stepping out a little bit so that the light fell on his face. He brushed blond hair out of his brilliant hazel eyes and smiled. He was dressed in an expensive suit and seemed unarmed.

Darian looked at the man's feet, searching for his shadow, but the man wasn't in the right spot for it; not enough light. "What problem is that?" Darian asked warily. The man was too well dressed to even be from here at all...he had to be one of those things. *They're everywhere,* Darian thought starting to back up slowly.

"Why, how to kill an angel of course," the man said, his relaxed posture throwing Darian off. "I, too, was wronged by those beings and have sought for years for the right tool to avenge that wrong." The man called Natasha opened his suit jacket, producing a red card and threw it at Darian with ease, the card fluttering effortlessly into his reach.

Darian stopped backing up and caught the card and looked up, but the man was gone. He looked at the card, turning it over in his shaking hands, and saw that there was a red side, and a black side; both identical. "Arnor's Desires" it read, listing an address here in Old Miami. There was a phone number as well as something called a fax number, whatever that was. Darian looked again at where the man used to be, shrugged, and walked out of the alley, new hope replacing his dour mood.

The Healer

She walked among the sick, a smile on her tired face, and encouraged them with her words of a better day. Raina placed her hand on one boy, his arm badly infected from a knife wound, and channeled her power slightly. The infection vanished like darkness in the light of dawn; the boy closed his eyes, restful sleep finally finding him. The woman that went by the name of Raina ran her pale hands through her bone-white hair and sat down, tears of frustration falling down her face from her silver eyes. She could instantly heal everyone here if she so chose, yet that would draw too much attention to what she was. The woman called Raina was slender and pale, dressed in a light rose sundress with a white belt. Though her hair was white, it was not her age that made it so; she appeared in her early thirties at best. Raina—or the archangel Raphael as she was known to her brothers and sisters—got back up and resumed her rounds, knowing that she couldn't save everyone at the improvised hospital.

The building in which the sick were being tended was a crumbling ruin that used to be a car factory, a remnant of the days when this area was a center for industry. Now, the side of the ruined center had a huge red cross painted on the side—surrounded by gang graffiti— and acted as a center for the sick and wounded trying to survive in Old Detroit. When humanity broke the world, many places of civilization fell quickly. This area fell to looting and riots more than anything else and now was home to gang wars and rivalries; the young and reckless were being recruited for the bangers' power moves.

"Sister Raina?" one of the other women asked, coming in with an urgent look on her face.

"Yes Greta? What is it?"

"There is a man here asking for you," Greta said, a look of concern on her weathered face.

"Is that a problem Greta? What has you worried so?" Raina asked, placing her hand on the woman's shoulder and channeling positive thoughts to the poor woman. She could do more than just heal wounds; she could even heal the soul if she had to.

"It's just...he said he was your brother and you've always said you were an only child," Greta admitted, wringing her hands together. "I fear he means ill towards you."

"Did he give a name?" the archangel asked warily, wondering if Michael had finally come to stop her meddling in the affairs of these mortals. He hated the fact that she used her powers so blatantly in front of them all; it was just one of Michael's rules for the archangels here walking among humanity...and the one she always broke.

"Yes, he said his name was Gabriel."

Raina let out a breath she didn't realize she had held and smiled warmly. "Thank you, Greta, you may show him in. Don't worry, he *is* like a brother to me," Raina said, her eyes dancing now. She hadn't seen the archangel Gabriel in almost ten years; it would do her good to lay eyes upon his visage once more. She walked toward the large window, as Greta went to let her visitor in, and looked up at the beautiful clouds drifting overhead. They parted and a single ray of brilliant sunshine came down to shine on her pale face.

I miss you too, Father, but these people need us so, she thought as a feeling of contentment washed over her instantly. She had always been the closest to Him out of all her brothers and sisters; even Michael. In fact, most of them never talked to Him anymore, claiming that He didn't listen. She knew better.

"You are a radiant example of *any* species dear sister," Gabriel said as he entered the room. He looked at the mortals as he passed them by and clicked his tongue. "Poor fellows, you're taking such good care of them for Father, aren't you?"

"It is good to see you too, Gabriel, and yes, someone has to." The archangel embraced her brother, feeling his warmth as he embraced her in return.

"I've been searching for you for a while Raina," Gabriel said, using the name she had taken to walk among the mortals. Some of them kept their originals, as the names didn't really stand out; others changed them to be more comfortable. "Though I confess, I never thought to start with Old Detroit." The archangel looked around once more; smoothing his white suit out of habit, then looked right at her and frowned. Finding each other was not easy, as they moved around constantly to avoid suspicion from the humans they were sent to guard and protect. Some of them had exchanged phone numbers, but a few had stayed off the radar so-to-speak.

"So, what do I owe the honor of this visit to, brother?" Raina asked as she bent down and placed a wet cloth on a patient's forehead.

"I need your help in mending an individual that I may have inadvertently scarred."

"Surely you didn't cause harm, Gabriel; you usually aren't violent. That's Aleksandr's province," she said, thinking of her dark-haired brother, Azrael. She walked towards the back motioning for him to follow.

"Not physically, no, but it happened nonetheless," Gabriel began, his hands behind his back as he walked once more with her. "He attacked me and in so doing caused the death of his mother. I couldn't bring her back, nor help his fractured mind. That is your area, I'm afraid."

"How long have you been searching for me?" she asked, knowing his answer would confirm her fear. She could indeed return the dead to life, but only in a certain amount of time. True resurrection had a time limit of three days.

"Alas, it has been months I'm afraid," Gabriel said, his eyes full of sorrow. "I also had to intervene in another mishap between Michael and Cain, of all people. Though thankfully I was only needed to encourage, not battle."

"What about Azrael bringing her soul back? Aren't you two close?"

"I did ask him, over coffee one day, but once the soul moves on there is nothing he can do," Gabriel confessed. He hung his head down almost like he was avoiding her gaze.

Raina lightly touched Gabriel's face, making him look into her soft eyes. "Well, let's go find this person so I can see what I can do to help."

"Thank you, sister."

The archangel Raphael gathered some supplies and let Greta know she had to leave for a bit, then she took Gabriel outside and into an alley so they could let their wings out. Gabriel's were a gorgeous two-tone white/brown, hers, an almost diaphanous silver. All archangels had wings that no one could see. They we're kept discorporate, almost inside of them. Both willed the wings to hide them and so it was that the two soaring beings flew over the city of Old Detroit unobserved and out across the heartlands, towards their destiny.

Weapon in Play

Darian stopped outside of the shop and looked about nervously; those angels could be anywhere. Opening the door and walking in, he noticed that the shop was empty despite being on the main strip of a lawless city. Every other shop was bustling with patrons, making deals and shifty transactions...yet this one was dead.

"Can I help ya, laddie?" A rough voice asked from behind the counter.

The accent was like old Scottish or maybe Welsh, yet Darian couldn't see anyone. The footsteps continued to sound from behind the counter though, like it was some kind of ghost. Right before Darian's nerve broke; a small figure popped up and rested on thick arms. The man was only about four feet tall and had a slight hunch to his back, standing on a stool so he could reach the counter.

"Yes, yes laddie. I'm a wee person, you can stop staring now," the man said, nodding his head. "My name is Arnor and I am here to sell you what you truly desire." The dwarf waved his arms out wide to take in all his collection, never taking his narrowed eyes off of Darian.

Darian looked around nervously and then back at the man called Arnor. He pulled out the card he was given and handed it to the man behind the counter, suddenly feeling empowered for some reason. "I was given this and told you have an item that could be used to help me," the young man said, and then he lowered his voice a bit and whispered. "I need to kill an angel."

"An angel you say! Whoa, big plans indeed. Tell old Arnor laddie, is it the fallen one you seek to injure?" The shop owner got down as he talked, walking behind a red curtain. The sound of rummaging and falling objects echoed throughout the store as he obviously searched for something.

"Fallen one? You mean Satan?"

"Aye, that's the one, though I've heard that he hates that particular name."

"No, this one's name is Gabriel," Darian said, remembering the name like it was yesterday. He had cursed that name for months, and now it was almost over.

"Really? Truly? Well, then, I have just the thing." Arnor pulled a vicious looking dagger made of weathered stone out of a sheath as he walked back and hopped up on his stool. Arnor slammed it down on the counter, making Darian jump, and laughed at the young man's reaction. "This here is the blade of Enmon and is made out of the stone tablets God himself supposedly gave to Moses. They, of course, fell to ruin after centuries and Enmon made a weapon out of them to slay the devil. It should technically work on any angelic being though."

"How much?" Darian asked, knowing that this may be out of his price range. He had a lot of money, but faced with the history and age of the seeming artifact in front of him, he might not have enough. He wasn't worried about it being authentic, he could feel the pulse of power from here—the same pulse he had felt when the angel lowered them to the floor all those months ago—it was a feeling he would never forget...

"For you laddie? The ring finger on your off hand," Arnor said in a serious tone. No smile, no joke, no smirk.

"You're kidding," Darian asked, looking down at his finger.

"Didn't ya notice there is no cash register in the shop? I don't take money, Laddie. I take things that people value," Arnor said, producing a rather sharp looking blade.

"Don't ya worry though; this blade seals the wound as it cuts, so you'll be fine."

"How?"

"Why, magic of course Laddie. Now, how about that payment?"

Darian placed his trembling hand on the counter and stared at the blade that would kill an angel. If the price was his finger, then so be it. His scream echoed off the walls as the blade sliced right through his finger and bit into the countertop. Darian pulled his hand back in agony, but Arnor was right, he wasn't bleeding at all.

"Here ya go, Laddie. One killing blade. Careful not to cut yerself."

Confrontation

Darian walked the dirty street in shock, looking down at his hand with a mixture of horror and awe. It hurt something awful, yet there was still no trace of blood. He hefted the stone dagger in his good hand and smiled; he was so close now. Darian saw the perfect place he was searching for, a small statue in the park near an open area. The parks were free of enforcers, usually, but were still monitored by some of the drug kings; it would be perfect for a meeting. He found an unoccupied bench, sat down, and closed his eyes. With the stone dagger behind his back, Darian prayed to Gabriel just like his mother had all those months ago. Darian squeezed his eyes shut harder as he called to the angel, pleading for him to hear him and come.

Baiting the angelic being with desperation in his thoughts; he needed the angel to come quickly before he lost what nerve he had. Finally, he heard the whoosh of air in front of him and smiled.

Raina heard the prayer even though it was addressed to Gabriel and knew that it was the boy, Darian.

"This way," Gabriel called out to Raina as he flew beside her. They were still over the fields of the old heartland, but at their speed they reached the flooded peninsula of Florida in less than fifteen minutes. They angled down towards Old Miami and saw the park and the boy sitting on a bench praying. They landed and folded their wings, approaching the boy slowly.

"I knew you'd come," Darian said, opening his eyes. Tears fell slowly from them as he stared at the two, something within them pulling at Raina's heart. The boy pulled a stone knife from behind his back and stood almost reverently.

"Hello Darian, I brought a friend to see you, and maybe help with your grief," Gabriel said.

Raina could feel the pulse of power in the weapon that the boy held. She knew then that it was a trap. "Careful, Gabriel," she whispered so that only he could hear her.

"Help me? I *begged* you to save my mom that day and you didn't!" Darian cried, tears streaming unabashedly. "You just flew off and *left* us there."

"I couldn't son. Your mother was already gone."

"You're an *angel* for Christ's sake!" Darian surged forward, brandishing the blade before him with very little skill.

Raina could almost feel the rage and grief emanating from the boy; "'Darian' is it?" Raina asked, stepping in front of Gabriel with her hands out. "I want to help now, all right?"

"Who are *you*?" the boy asked, swinging the blade back and forth between the two archangels.

"My name is Raina and I'm a healer," she started, walking slowly. "I want to help, but you have to put down the blade before I can do that," Raina said, focusing her power into the boy's mind. The damaged mind before her was a jumble of pain, hate, and guilt. She could feel that what he had accidentally done, he blamed on Gabriel. Yet deep down, the boy knew that it was his own fault his mother died. *It is literally tearing his mind apart,* she thought as she stepped closer.

"I...can you can bring her back?" Darian asked, his watery eyes looking at her with hope.

There was such light in those eyes that Raina felt her own tears starting to fall, the silver drops gliding down her face. "Yes, Darian, I can," she lied, knowing that once she was done, he would be whole once more. That was the only good thing about not having a soul. The morality was taken out of the equation for beings like her.

Raina watched as the boy dropped the stone blade, then stepped in and placed her hands on his face, sending her healing into his mind. She looked over at Gabriel, his guilt obvious on his face, yet he smiled at her anyway.

"I...feel her," Darian said softly, closing his eyes. He wept openly now, great sobs as the angel held his face in her two hands. "She's at peace."

"As are you, now, my little one. Go through life without guilt or shame; those memories are purged from you," The archangel Raphael let go of the boy and hugged him, her tears falling on his shoulder. "You have a fresh new start now. Go now and live your life how she would've wanted you to."

Gabriel placed his hand upon his sister's shoulder and nodded his thanks.

Raina released Darian and looked down to pick up the blade, but it had vanished. *No matter, it probably went back to where it came from*, she thought. *Such is the way of some of the powerful artifacts.* As the young boy stumbled away, Raina and Gabriel unfolded their wings and left him, whole and at peace for the first time in months.

Plans

The man known as Natasha sat back from his desk and spun the stone blade in his hands, feeling the pulse of power that could very well end his existence here on earth for good. He had been trying to get his hands on this weapon for many years, but stubborn old Arnor would never give it up. Lucifer laughed as he placed the dangerous artifact back in its sheath. He stood and walked over to the wall, opening a concealed door and placing it with some of the other objects he had collected over the years. He shut the door once more and smiled. He had snuck right under his siblings' noses and taken it whilst they were busy healing that horribly fractured soul. Very predictable indeed. This knife was special though, it was going to play a major part in his ongoing plans.

The fallen angel Lucifer sat back at his desk once more and let his wings out, the glorious, white, feathers betraying his dark heart—or so they always said. He laughed again and plotted his next move, one which would see his family torn asunder at last, yet not in the way they would think.

Learning how to Love

MEMORIES OF THE FALL

Michael's chest heaved with air as he stood up, golden hair falling over broad shoulders as he caught his breath. *That fight was harder than it should've been,* he thought as he scanned the horizon for any stragglers. He looked around for his weapon, the sword that had flown from his hands mid-battle. It stood among the clouds, stuck like it was buried into the very earth, its flames still slowly flickering along its silver blade. Thankfully he had dropped it, for if he had it near the end, he may have ended his brother's life instead of throwing him down; *that* wouldn't have gone over well with Father at all. He spread his bright white wings, flexing the right one where Lucifer had slashed it, wincing at the pain. It would heal in minutes, but it still hurt.

"Art thou all right, brother?"

"Yes, Gabriel, I'm fine. *Thank* you for taking care of his followers whilst *I* banished *our* brother," Michael said, sarcasm dripping from his angelic mouth. He had been the one to finally challenge his brother over his behavior. After hearing his excuses as to why Lucifer rebelled against Father, the angel of battle decided to cast him out of heaven. It had, of course, caused an all-out war with the host of angels that had sided with the errant miscreant...

"Don't take that tone with *me,* brother. *You* started this all by yourself. Father said to leave them be, but what is done cannot be undone," Gabriel said as he walked away. "By the way, He wants a word," the messenger of God said, his dirty blond hair swirling around his two-toned white/brown wings.

"You didn't have to cast him down, you know," a small voice said from behind Michael. Raphael was on the ground, her silver tears spilling over broken wings as she held an angel in her arms. Several were lying dead or broken—those that refused to flee after Lucifer had been thrown down upon the earth—as the archangel of life grieved. Her bone white hair was in her face, blood staining her robes and hands, as she held the lifeless Hanandiel.

The sight gave Michael pause. "I...had no choice from where I stood, Raph. I'm sorry."

"From where you stood?" she asked incredulously, her voice gaining volume finally. "Michael, you always stand so that all can see you. Sometimes that obscures your vision of things, mainly because you're looking at yourself," Raphael finished, anger showing in her normally soft voice. "All he wanted was to be loved as much as these humans Father is going to create. Was that too much to ask?"

"*He was ever the favorite!*" Michael screamed back at her, his temper once more getting the best of him. He was quickly losing what patience he had left. "He sat at the very feet of God, swooned over because he was the Light of this place. He had no *right!*"

"*Enough, Michael.*" The warning voice of God reverberated throughout the entire realm, shaking the archangel of battle to his very core...

Michael opened his eyes, the memory of that time, eons ago, shocking him back to reality. As an archangel he didn't need to sleep, but lately he had been dozing off here and there—a side effect of mimicking humanity for so long.

"Are you alright, Father Michael?" a man's voice asked next to him.

Michael looked over, trying to smile, though the awful memory had shaken him to his core. Even the memory of Father's voice was enough to do that to a powerful being such as him. "Yes, just a bad dream is all." He stood and brushed off his black clothes then adjusted his white collar. To these humans he was a priest, though it wasn't far from the truth. Michael continued across the sands of the broken city, walking past the people and nodding as they gave him space. Everyone that had survived the Fall of Arizona had become very religious, so they revered the coming of a priest. Rumors of Satan himself walking the streets here had grabbed his attention, so he had come all the way from the east coast to the ruins of Phoenix searching for his fallen brother, vowing to stop him once and for all.

Old Grudges

The man called Natasha sat back in the hot, arid breeze and waved his hand at the waitress. He watched her saunter over, hips swinging in her short sundress, letting his lurid thoughts drift. He brushed his blond hair out of his brilliant hazel eyes as she stopped in front of him, her own eyes roaming lavishly over his Armani suit, complete with silver cufflinks.

"Another round, sir?" the waitress asked, smiling seductively. "Or is there something *else* I could do for you?"

"I would normally indulge you on that offer—at least twice—but alas, I have an appointment with a family member who should be here any minute," he said as he looked around the ramshackle establishment sitting in the dead center of the Ruins of Phoenix. The sand was being carried in through the massive holes in the walls by the hot, dry air. "I will, however, have another Bloody Mary." Natasha watched her walk away for a minute with a wistful look, then went back to the task at hand—keeping an eye out for Michael. He knew that his brother was coming—he had made enough of a scene, after all—and hopefully the first part of his plan would finally fall into place.

"You're a little out of place, friend," a rough voice said from behind him.

"Well, I didn't plan on the dress code being so...apocalyptic." Natasha turned slowly to look at the owner of the voice and almost laughed. The man was well over six feet tall and his ragged coat barely stayed on his massive frame. The clothes underneath were patched and frayed but looked better than the man's face. That face was burned and scarred—likely due to the after effects of the Fall of Arizona, no doubt—and he favored one leg.

Arizona had been hit the worst, fallout annihilating most of the arid state. Phoenix was the only thing that barely survived—if you wanted to call this surviving. The people that made this ruined city their home were scarred and broken; most of the children born now had deformities. Why anyone choose to live here amazed the fallen angel, yet they continued to do so.

"Oh, a smart ass..." the big man started to say, cracking his knuckles, but stopped as Natasha stood, straightened his suit, and looked the man dead in the eye without so much as a wink. Something had changed in the room and everyone quieted at once.

"I have a problem to attend to, so I will let this go, for now," Natasha said, eyes blazing for just the big man to see. "Besides, I believe that your current wife is with your cousin at the moment and I'm sure there are no clothes involved. You might want to go find them and put that temper to good use."

"Lucifer!" a deep voice boomed from the other side of the room.

Natasha, or Lucifer as his family liked to call him, sighed as the scared man retreated in a mix of wonder and fear. "Now see what you've done?" he called after the man. "You've distracted me and I missed my brother's grand entrance." Natasha turned and saw the priest in the doorway, the other people giving him a wide berth, bowing. "Oh, he's not *really* a priest, people," Lucifer said, walking around a table to keep Michael at bay for the moment. "And I go by Natasha these days." He sent out a silent prayer then, so Michael wouldn't pick up on it, calling upon an ally that he needed for this to work. He just hoped they showed up in time.

"I don't care what these people call you, brother, your evil stops here," Michael said as the people rushed out of the ruined bar. They knew that something wasn't quite right and after all they had been through over the last couple of decades, they knew when to take shelter.

"Evil?" Lucifer asked as he backed up, drawing the stone knife slowly. The artifact throbbed with power, something Michael could no doubt feel from where he stood. "What evil have I done *this* time, dear brother?"

Michael stopped, staring at the blade in horror. "Is that the blade of Enmon?" the archangel of battle asked, fear and hatred flashing across his face.

Lucifer laughed and waved it in the air for show. "Made out of the stone tablets Father himself gave to Moses," he said, circling around the table that wouldn't truly stop either one of them if it came to it. "Enmon made this out of those very tablets to slay me, though it should technically work on any angel, in theory of course."

"You're no angel Lucifer; you fell from grace eons ago..." Michael said, but was cut off by Lucifer's sudden rage.

"*I was pushed*!" the fallen angel cried, throwing the table aside with his free hand, the flimsy wooden object sailing through the air at least forty feet and crashing into the ruined wall. "You know that very well, *brother*, since it was you that pushed me down." Lucifer advanced upon his brother, his normally hazel eyes burning like green flame. The time was now, all or nothing.

Gone Too Far

"So now you'll kill me?" Michael asked, wondering if. Indeed, that blade could do what his nefarious brother claimed. "You know I'm the better fighter, Lucifer, you can't win."

"I'm counting on it, Michael," Lucifer said, lunging as he let his white, majestic wings unfold, blowing dust in a circle around him.

Michael unfurled his bright, white wings, as well, dodging the thrust and grabbing Lucifer's arm and throwing him across the room. They dodged and parried for what seemed like hours, though it wasn't that long at all. Suddenly, Lucifer lunged recklessly and Michael caught the wrist holding the blade. He twisted and spun, wrenching the blade from his brother's grasp, and slamming it into the chest of the fallen angel. The very air around them burst, like a concussion without sound, blowing everything away from them in a fifty-foot radius. Lucifer fell to the floor, gasping weakly as the powerful blade stuck out from his chest. Thankfully, no one could witness this because of their wings being out...not that anyone stuck around for the show; the people of Phoenix had seen enough already.

"*No!*" the cry echoed throughout the room, originating from the blasted doorway. A woman, slender and pale, stood crying silver tears. She had bone white hair and was dressed in a light rose sundress, her diaphanous silver wings a sight to behold, angel or not.

"Raphael... he came at me and I..." Michael started to say, standing in her way as she ran to Lucifer.

The archangel Raphael threw up her arm with everything she had, backhanding Michael out of the way, the full force of her ire behind the strike. Michael hit the far wall and stood in an instant, rushing back to stop her. "You can't Raph...he's evil," he tried explaining, but her eyes stopped him cold—eyes that said he had gone too far.

"Sister...you came?" Lucifer asked with barely any strength. His words were almost a whisper as the blade pulsed in his chest.

"I heard your prayer, brother, and I came as fast as the wind could carry me. I'm here," Raphael said, closing her eyes and placing her hand on Lucifer's chest. Her silver tears fell as her now glowing hand disintegrated the blade and slowly closed the vicious wound.

"What have you done?" Michael cried, advancing again. "I had finally ended this and you go and bring him back? Why?"

"Because he is my brother...*our* brother...and I love him!" the archangel of life said defiantly, standing up and blocking the way to Lucifer. "As should *you*."

Michael seethed with anger, his wings trembling with barely constrained rage. "For this you shall be cast out with him, sister," he growled, stealing himself to do what he must. He grabbed her in both hands, surprising her, and lifted her high.

"Enough, Michael. Leave your sister be."

The voice echoed in their heads, loud enough to drop both archangels to their knees, making them close their eyes and breathe through it.

Lucifer didn't seem to be affected as he sat up slowly, rubbing his chest. "Now you've done it, Michael..." Lucifer said, as he struggled to his feet. "...and you owe me a new suit too."

Michael sat there, crying in frustration, his tears mingling with the blood on his hands as he wiped them away. "Don't you see? I *do* love him; that's why this hurts so much." He stood, stumbling away until he got to the door. His actions finally bashing through to his head as he tried to clear his head. He had tried to kill his brother... *Am I no better than Cain?* he asked himself, turning and looking at them, tears still falling. "I loved him and he was going to hurt Father. For that, yes, I would kill my brother; never think that I do not love him, though."

Lucifer leaned on the wall, smiling at his sister. "I can't believe you hit him that hard," he said, laughing though the pain. She had healed most of the wound, but Dad was it still sore.

"He would've thrown me down, too," Raphael said, folding her wings and looking up at the ceiling.

"Yes, but Father always loved you best," Lucifer lied. "Still, I didn't see that coming; the big guy himself intervening."

"You knew," she accused, standing and turning on him with those eyes. "You knew he would try and kill you. That's why you called me, prayed for me, to come help you."

'I've always told you that he was a monster, and now you know it to be true." Lucifer put away his wings as well, as people started coming in to see what had happened. He knew she would be angry with him, in truth he was expecting it, but he also knew that once she had time to think that she would come around and forgive him. The best part was that she had destroyed the only thing on earth that could've killed him. "Still, I can't wait to tell Azrael about your wicked backhand," Lucifer said to break the growing tension.

Raphael shook her head and tried not to smile, but failed in the end. "You always could make me laugh, Lucifer."

"Natasha, please, *Raina.*" Natasha added to make a point. "And you said you loved me," he added, holding his heart in mock surprise.

"Oh, shut up," she chided as the people came in with awe on their faces. The two siblings walked out of the place together, the man called Natasha and the healer known as Raina-brother and sister.

Remembering the End

Michael walked numbly to the edge of the ruined town, his wings still out and his head hung down. *How had it come to this again*, he thought as he beat his wings soaring towards the sun through the clouds, thinking back to that fateful day once more...

"Enough, Michael." The warning voice of God reverberated throughout the entire realm, shaking the archangel of battle to his very core...

Michael looked down at his hands, hands that had beaten his brother bloody a few minutes earlier. How had it come to this? They were so close just a few centuries before.

"How many went with him?" a quiet voice asked at his side.

Michael looked down at Ariel, the archangel of nature and sighed. "I counted at least twenty and five that leapt after their leader. Sadly, they were only lesser angels, so they *fell* instead," he replied, still thinking of what he was going to say to Father. When an angel *fell* they actually lost their wings, their bodies sometimes melting away or deforming. Others changed completely, their bodies adapting, but they were the minority.

"They will hit very hard indeed without their wings, and some may never be the same," Ariel said, holding back tears of her own. "Do we know any of them?"

"Mephistopheles, Asmodeus, and Lilith," he said sadly. *Oh, how heaven will miss Lilith's laugh,* he thought as he realized how badly she could be twisted by the fall. That thought almost made his own tears fall, yet he straightened his back and shook his head. *No, I won't cry for those traitors.*

"I think I saw Nergal and Belial, as well," another voice said coming up out of nowhere.

"Uriel, I wasn't aware you were even *here* during the battle," Michael admonished, staring down the archangel of knowledge.

"I had him come in my stead," a strong voice said, appearing out of thin air. He had raven black hair and black wings, along with a wicked, curved blade.

"We missed your blade during the battle, Azrael," Michael said, a hint of accusation in his voice. The two had never truly gotten along, a strong sense of competition dividing them since the beginning.

"*I* was protecting the throne, a job *you* were supposed to be doing," the archangel of death said, his tone one of challenge...

"I *was*!" Michael shouted, the very clouds beneath them shaking with the power behind his voice.

"*I said, 'enough'.*"

Michael froze, his ire burning in his chest. *I have to get this over with and calm down*, he thought, willing himself to the throne of God. He appeared before the massive throne of marble and immediately dropped to his knees; to his horror, it was empty. "Father? Father I am sorry but I did this to protect you," he said, looking everywhere. As he stood, searching, a small light appeared on the throne, burning letters into the marble. The archangel read them and cried finally, his ire melting away at last.

Son, Take Azrael and go to earth and watch my new creation as they grow. They will have something you do not, so it is your task to learn. Once you have learned the most important lesson, only then may you come home.

The letters blazed then vanished as Michael stood staring. "What do they have father?" he asked, a feeling of loss creeping into his chest. "And what could I possibly learn from them?" Letters blazed once more, faster this time, and he could not understand the meaning.

They have a soul, my child, and I want you to understand what that means.

Michael stood and suddenly he was out in the fields again, the throne gone. He would go and take Azrael to earth, but he doubted he would ever learn from these new humans...

Michael came out of his reverie, his tears finally stopping. *Love,* he thought, *how can these creatures show me what I already know?* Yet as he tried to fly towards heaven, a place of thought and will, he was still denied. It was then he realized what he was missing. Raphael hadn't tried to stop him from casting her down; he had grabbed her effortlessly. She had stood in the way of him and Lucifer, knowing that she would pay the ultimate price. She truly did love him. *Is that what I've been missing? Is it the forgiveness of love that I have failed to embrace?* Lost in thought, Michael never saw the sky blur and shift, the clouds giving way to his true home. "It wasn't the humans that would teach me, it was Raphael," he said to no one in particular as he landed upon the clouds. *She and my fallen brother... Oh, Lucifer. I am sorry I have hated you all these*

eons, he thought as he came to realize finally what his Father had always tried to teach every one of them.

"Welcome home, son."

Act II:

Pieces on the Board

"And I say to you, God has called us to reckoning and we have been found wanting" — Archbishop Frederick Valencio. Nine months after the calamity in the ruins of the Vatican.

Fallen Angel Scorned

Dangerous Woman

The woman walked into the club, the pounding music thumping in her chest. Every eye turned towards her, their gazes lingering as she passed them. She was stunning, her figure enticing, as she pushed her way through the throng of bodies. Yet, she only had eyes for the live band up on the stage. The fallen angel, Lilith, sauntered over to the front of the raised platform, her long black hair matching her black silk dress. That dress—cut up her legs almost to her waist—showed more skin than most women in here had and matched the twin pools of tar that were her eyes.

"Hey lady, did it hurt?" an awkward voice asked over the loud music. The kid reeked of alcohol, swaying on his feet as he alternated staring at her tits and her face.

"Did what hurt, lovely?" Lilith asked, knowing full well what was coming. She didn't have to shout to be heard; such was the power of her kind. If she wanted someone to hear her, they did.

"When you fell from heaven?" the kid asked, leaning on one of the support posts and almost missing. "You know...cause you're an angel?"

"Actually, yes, it did hurt. You see, after Lucifer was cast down, those of us that were loyal knew that we would be punished, so we leapt after him," she started, holding his gaze with her own. The kid didn't stand a chance against her will and she could feel his lust growing. "However, we weren't archangels, so our wings ignited, burning away as we fell, hurtling towards earth and hitting with such force that craters formed where our broken bodies lay. I hit somewhere in what you would call Australia. Sadly, though, you people know us more as demons, now, than angels."

"Um...ok, well I gotta..." The kid tried to tear himself away, his mind knowing he was in danger, yet his will wasn't strong enough; even his words died away as his eyes started to gloss over.

"Don't you want to know what I have instead of wings?" she asked, her voice purring in his ear as she came closer. "Like angel wings, they can't be seen unless I want you to see them. *Unlike* angel wings you can still see me when I do."

"What...what do you have?" he asked, unable to stop himself. His voice was tinged with fear and apprehension, his whole body starting to shake now.

"Feel me...right here," she said, guiding his hands to her hair. His hands went through her glossy black strands, and she felt him freeze as he hit her horns. "Aren't they pretty?" Lilith asked as she let him see them then as well, the look on his face telling her that he was completely broken. His now-vacant eyes were locked on the curling horns that spread out from her head. She had grown them out of her burnt wing stalks on her back, and even helped some of the others grow theirs as well. All except poor Nergal and Belial. Nergal and Belial lost their entire bodies-so lived on only as spirits these days, able to possess others, but not for very long.

Lilith took the young man aside, remembering why she was here. "Now, stay here until I'm finished." She danced her way back to the stage, looking at the singer with hungry eyes. The man was dressed in faded jeans and a tight white t-shirt. He had a jacket that looked worn and very old, like it was his grandfather's, and his piercing eyes were the color of wet dirt; a deep brown that seemed made of the very earth itself. He had long brown hair and tanned skin on a massive frame filled with corded muscle.

"We all follow the rules and fail
We all try our hardest and fall
Yet how are we supposed to learn
If God hates us all"
"Walk the earth, fight the pain
Live forever
Every day the same"

The band was called Eden's Promise and they were gaining popularity here in New Dallas, yet she knew these songs already. She had heard the man sing them differently centuries ago. Once the song was done, she whistled loudly, like everyone else, yet the singer heard her and looked, his eyebrows furrowing.

"Thanks folks! Be back next week," the man said, rushing off the stage.

Lilith walked over to where the exit was with her new toy, the kid drooling now as he stared at the floor, yet there was no sign of her prey. "Damn him...strike that; already been done," she said out loud, her frustration clear to anyone paying attention. "Well, young morsel, let's go sate my appetite and then I'll worry about finding him again."

Lilith walked back on the dance floor as the house music played, swaying her hips, and letting her power radiate out slowly. All angels had something they could do, and when she fell, hers changed. She used to have such a laugh, and at times she could bring joy to almost anyone, even that stuffy archangel, Michael. When she fell, her form, and indeed her very being, twisted. Now instead of pure joy and laughter, she could bring lust and longing. Now her power went out to fuel the people around her into fits of passion. She lived vicariously through them, unable to find solace in the acts herself. *Dance my pets, the night is young.*

ᴺEW SURROUNDINGS

The bear let out a roar of contention, shaking its head at the slight woman. Ariel raised her hand, letting her feelings flow out towards the animal, and smiled. "Hush now, I'm here," she said, pulling the thorn out of its neck and sending calming energy into the thick fur as it roared again. "There, you big baby." It nuzzled her and lumbered away. *I never knew what I was missing,* she thought as she walked through the dense forest, passing between the ancient trees and brushing them with her fingers; her emerald eyes half closed in bliss.

Ariel was the archangel of nature and had spent the eons in heaven watching over humanity and her own children; the creatures of myth and legend. When humanity broke the world, Gabriel, Raphael, and Jophiel came down to join Michael and Azrael in helping humanity. She and Uriel had stayed in heaven, but now she was here, walking among them, learning from them, as did another of her brothers not so long ago.

Michael was home now and he had sent her down here in his steed with an important mission. One she hadn't been able to locate as yet. She ran her fingers through her long brown hair, strands the color of the very earth she walked upon, and sighed. She had to find Cain and make sure he was staying out of trouble. She found the clearing and looked up, the sun barely visible on the horizon as it set for the night. She smoothed her green shawl and grabbed her new phone out of her faded jeans and hit the call button, dialing her other brother.

"Why, hello sister. Are you finally learning how to work this technology?" Gabriel asked on the other end of the device. His voice was clear and concise, like he was standing right here.

"Well, I didn't really have a choice. It was either this, or fly after you all the time," she joked, letting her deep brown wings out and shaking them. The cool evening breeze came through the trees and washed over her wings gently; they felt so good in the wind like this.

"So, what can I do for you?"

"I know I said I wanted to do this on my own, but I've been to New Seattle, Old Miami, and now here to the New England City States and I can't find Cain anywhere." Ariel marveled at how close they had all become since the years after Michael's ascension to heaven once more. Where at first, they had gone for decades without seeing one another, they all had these new phones to keep in touch. It was Azrael's idea, of course, and she loved the idea of being close again.

"I see Michael wants you to keep tabs on him?" Gabriel laughed. "Well, you are in luck. I do happen to know where he is at the moment."

"Where?"

"He's in New Dallas, playing in a band called Eden's Promise. He resurrects the band every fifty years or so to avoid attention. He's quite talented."

"Seriously?" Ariel asked, the irony hilarious to her. "You go to his concerts?"

"I'm always serious, my dear, I just enjoy things more than most," Gabriel said, his tone growing a bit more serious. "But no, I haven't seen or heard about him since the debacle at Mercy General, almost ten years ago." The line was quiet for a moment, awkward silence telling her something else was coming. "I have to warn you, though, if Michael said anything about hurting him, Father has forbidden it."

"Oh, I'm aware. Thank you, Gabriel." She hit the red button and slipped he phone into her tight jeans once more, taking flight up through the clearing and into the sky above the Forest of Vermont, its green trees falling away below her as she soared into the clouds.

It was almost midnight when Ariel made it to New Dallas, flying down to the neon city and bypassing its high stone walls. This massive city state was one of the more economically sound places in the new world, being kept safe by the Rangers of old. They had built high stone walls when the worst came down, and limited entrance to refugees. It was a hard call, but in the end the city state prospered and grew. Ariel hadn't been in any rush and so took her time seeing the city from high above and reveling in its nighttime glory; flashing neon lights called to human desires of any flavor.

Ariel kept her wings out as she walked to avoid the people hurrying to and from dark places this late at night, waiting until she was hidden from public view until she folded them away. So it was that she found herself in an alley as the target of her search ran right at her. Thankfully, since Cain was cursed, he could see her even with her wings out. "Cain, wait."

The man pulled up short, a panicked look on his weathered face. "Alright, which one are you?" Cain asked, his whole demeanor shouting violence.

"I'm Ariel, archangel of nature and Michael told me to just check up on you," she said, a little taken aback. The sheer violence in the man's stance made her jumpy, to say the least. She had watched humanity from above for eons, even watched this man from time to time, yet nothing prepared her for being this close to him.

Cain was the first murderer, killer of his brother Abel. As such he was cursed by God to be a vagrant and a wanderer on the earth. He was given a mark by God so that none may do him harm, essentially letting him live forever, and never letting him fully pass on. Unfortunately, the rage that started all this was still within him and was passed to his male progeny.

"Check up on me?" Cain laughed right in her face; his cold smile didn't seem to touch his narrowed eyes, eyes that said he had seen everything and didn't like any of it.

"I promise. That's all he said," Ariel replied with her hands out to her side. The archangel stepped closer, his smell intriguing her; it was almost like the musk of an animal. This close, she realized he was a perfect specimen of humanity, Tall and broad-his frame was packed with muscle, yet it was his deep brown eyes pulling her into his very soul that seemed to draw her. She had never felt like this before, and had no idea what it was.

"You mean you're not going to try and kill me?"

"Not at all, and it wouldn't work anyway."

"Oh, it would work—and trust me, I feel it every time— but I just end up coming back after a while," Cain said looking down at her.

Ariel stepped even closer—a hair's breadth away from the man now—and laid her hand on him like she would any animal she was trying to calm; it did not have the effect she wanted it to have. A charge ran through her, from her feet to her head, and filled her with...well, she wasn't sure. It must've had the same effect on him because he backed away like he had seen a ghost, his hand clutching where she had touched him.

"What?" they both echoed. Before either of them could speak about the event, a scream split the night as a woman came around the back corner of the alley, heading right for them.

HORNS OF JEALOUSY

"You thought you could just run out on me?" Lilith screamed as she stormed down the alley towards him. He could change his name to Adam, and buy new clothes, but he would always be the same old Cain to her. "After all these decades searching for you?"

"Lilith, when I left you in London, I meant what I said. You and I are *bad* for each other." Cain turned and stood protectively in front of another woman, his massive frame almost obscuring her completely.

"It was the nineteenth century; I thought it was just the atmosphere of the impoverished making you weary of me." Lilith slowed her stride as she neared, turning on her power to lure him in. Somehow it wasn't having the effect it usually did on him. "What's new? What have you done?" the fallen angel asked, her mood shifting quickly. Her eyes went to the woman behind him, something about her seemed familiar...

"It wasn't the atmosphere, Lilith, it was you. Whenever we are together my rage boils up and takes over. I killed all those people, just because you asked me to." Cain's chest was heaving now, his rage slowly bubbling up to the surface just being near her.

The woman behind him stepped out, her stance balanced and ready. "It's been a long time, Lilith. It's good to see you've got your looks back at least, if not you disposition." It looked like the woman was going to say more, but something seemed to click behind her eyes and she turned towards Cain. "Wait...eighteen hundreds London? Cain, were you Jack the Ripper?"

"It's not something I am proud of, Ariel," Cain said, "and please call me Adam."

That was where she knew the girl from...It was the archangel Ariel! That angel always had her head in the animal world, dealing with her special children. The humans called them cryptids now—just a fancy word for myth and mystery. "This is between us, *Ariel*, you can just go back to your little forest and fuck bigfoot." Lilith walked up and poked Cain in the chest with one long finger, her nail piercing his shirt. "As for you..." Lilith never finished the sentence as a wind picked her up and blew her back. She stumbled and caught her balance, seeing Ariel right in front of Lilith's former lover.

"Lilith, please don't make this hard," Ariel warned, her wings out now and a gnarled wooden staff in her hands out of nowhere. "I'm here to keep an eye on Adam, and I won't let you corrupt him again."

Lilith was furious, her horns throbbing and steam coming off of her skin. "You think you can take him from *me*?" She flared her horns out and crouched, ready for a fight. Before she could act, Cain was there, lifting Lilith off the ground by her neck and pushing Ariel back towards the street.

"Stop!" Cain roared, throwing the fallen angel back into the alley with one arm. He was taking great breaths in, trying to stay calm, but the rage was growing.

"Yes, Cain, let it out! Embrace the rage and we can be together once more!" Lilith knew that if he killed again she could keep him by her side forever. Cain was all she had since Lucifer left her centuries ago—dropped like an old broken toy. The others wouldn't talk to her and Asmodeus openly hated her. Lilith had remade herself, her body beautiful once more by draining these humans of their passion and vitality, yet it only lasted a couple years before she had to do it again.

"Cain...Adam," Ariel corrected herself, stepping towards him again, her staff gone from her hands once more. With her wings out she seemed like a glorious angel next to the ancient murderer. "You don't want to do this. I can help you," Ariel said softly, her voice calm and tender, making Lilith sick to her stomach.

"I..."

Ariel reached out and laid her hand on his heaving chest as his hands clenched and unclenched into fists at his sides. "Feel the power of calm, old one, and be at ease."

Something happened then, a concussion without sound, and Lilith was blown farther back into the alley, slamming into an overflowing dumpster. Garbage rained down on her as she stood with furious rage, her dress and hair littered with refuse. She screamed her own rage at the affront, but the both of them had disappeared. *Run all you want Cain, I'll find you and then we will be together once more,* she thought as she stomped out of the alley to her car. *And you, Ariel... you will wish you were still in heaven when I'm done with you.*

Ariel landed— in what the signs said was Highland Park—with the big man in her arms, most of her clothes tattered from the blast. The archangel had poured her calm into Cain's rage and the two opposing forces met concussively, blowing out from them with such force that it overturned cars and blew out nearby windows. Ariel had grabbed him and flown off before Lilith could get her bearings; Ariel had no intention of fighting her fallen sister unless she had to. It still left a very awkward conversation, though, and it didn't help that she was mostly naked.

"What did you do to me?" Cain asked, holding his head, and leaning against a tree. His clothes looked just as tattered, but she didn't mind at all.

"I'm sorry, Adam. I just tried to calm you like I do with some of the wilder animals," Ariel confessed, wrapping her wings around herself as she tried not to stare at the masculine man before her. *What is coming over me?* she thought as she looked down at her feet.

"Don't be sorry. Whatever you did, it worked." The man going by the name of Adam stood and offered his hand. "Now, let's go get you some clothes before that green-eyed demon can find us again."

Ariel laughed at the term most of humanity had come to call the angels that had fallen so many eons ago.

"You might need some clothes too," Ariel said with a blush, still covering herself with her wings.

Adam took his tattered jacket and placed it around her shoulders with a gentle smile. "We can grab some once we figure out where we're going," he said.

"How do you feel about lots of trees?" Ariel asked, knowing the perfect spot for them to relax and lay low. *It has nothing to do with how attractive he is either*, she tried to convince herself.

"I'd love to." Adam walked towards her and smiled, "But let's drive, you could use the rest and we have a couple things to discuss," he said.

Ariel folded her wings and walked with him out of the park, a smile on her face that she couldn't make go away.

EPILOGUE

The man watched the fallen angel get into her car, a sleek black speed machine that fit her personality perfectly. He brushed his slick blond hair out of his brilliant hazel eyes and smiled; it was going splendidly. The man known as Natasha was dressed in an Armani suit, complete with silver cuff links, and he walked back into the club after Lilith drove away. It had been years since he had started all this, but he had never forgotten his long game. He had told Lilith where to find Cain, just like he had sent Gabriel the message as to what band was playing here tonight.

"Invitation only, bud," the bouncer at the door said as he approached.

"Oh, I assure you my name will be on that list. Name's Natasha."

"What kind of a man has the name Natasha?"

"The kind that pays bouncers to put said name on the list," Natasha said, slipping two hundred-dollar bills into the man's chest pocket. The fallen archangel, Lucifer, walked right past the man and into the club. *Now that Cain and Lilith are out of the way, I can get to his progeny without interruption. Besides, Ariel will keep that man busy for years, especially with Lilith chasing after them.*

The Children of Destiny

THE PROBLEM

He walked across the semi-flooded street with measured, angry steps, splashing everyone he passed, yet he hardly noticed because of his foul mood. It was alright though; everyone that lived here was used to the constant water flowing into Old California Island. When the world broke, the fault line under California shattered and sunk most of the state, flooding the major cities if not completely submerging them. What was left was a large island with waterlogged streets and wooden walkways. Tourists flocked here to see the underwater buildings and statues that remain in the crystal-clear waters.

The man flipped his long, dirty blond hair out of his emerald green eyes, and weaved through the crowd of youngsters. Gabriel brushed the beaded moisture off of his white suit and muttered to himself about personal space as the tourists kept walking, staring about the ruined city with awe. Sometimes he hated mortals. His name was Gabriel, and he was an archangel, sent by God to watch over humanity after they broke their world with their toys of destruction. There were several other siblings of his on earth, as well as the lesser angels all around the globe, but they hadn't really been in touch until the last thirty years or so. His fellow brothers and sisters took it upon themselves to answer the prayers of the beleaguered when they could, and to keep a lid on things that others—his brother Lucifer for instance—may interfere with. Gabriel sighed at the thought of his fallen brother. He didn't hate him, not like Michael had, but the devil was a pain in the wings sometimes.

"Hey, man you have a quarter?" a man asked, sitting on a soaked mattress holding out a pan with a good amount of change in it. He seemed like your normal beggar, yet there was something off.

Gabriel stopped and looked at the man, scrutinizing every aspect of the situation. Not only was he the archangel tasked as God's messenger, he was also very adept at spotting lies. The supposed beggar appeared homeless, yet his shoes weren't wet enough for the sinking island which he was on, and his hands weren't wrinkled as everyone else's. "Tell me, dear child," Gabriel said, leaning down and staring into the charlatan's eyes. "Do you believe that there are beings that can punish mortals in God's name?"

"Hey, man, it's no thing, jus' wanted a quarter is all." The man stood easily, collected his belongings, and started to walk away.

Gabriel grabbed the charlatan's collar and picked him up off of the ground with ease. This was impressive because Gabriel wasn't really a big man at all. He was a little over five feet tall, while the man was easily six feet and over two hundred pounds. The archangel held him up without even shaking-smiling at the man's shocked expression. Gabriel was never one for violence—that was Michael's thing—but he did have a thing for justice.

"Well, you see, I am one of those beings. And if you don't stop scamming these tourists of their money, I will personally bring you before God Himself," Gabriel warned. The man nodded his head slowly; Gabriel dropped him in the street, water splashing everywhere as the man scrambled away. Gabriel held onto the pan of money as the man took off across the watery street and shrugged. The archangel turned and threw the money into the air, the change splashing into the one-inch-deep water as people hurried to see how much there was and if they could grab some.

He moved on, bigger problems on his mind than beggars. Father had sent him a dream-like vision of a prophesy put into motion somehow and he had to find out how to stop it. It was flashes of darkness and light, much like what had fractured the world years ago, but ascended into heaven. Gabriel remembered Lucifer's uprising, and had no desire to bring that kind of war back to the Silver realm. He recited the prophetic dream to himself once more as he walked toward the old church he had come here for:

— And lo, the child of Cain, cured and whole, will bare his soul to the Seer and there will be an

explosion. Light will shine on the children of destiny, but not before the best of God's servant's fall from grace into darkness, coming to regret everything. —

Gabriel arrived at the ruined doors of the Cathedral of Our Lady of the Angels and paused, bowing his head. Though the Roman Catholics had gotten a bunch of things wrong, they did know how to build a proper cathedral. The building survived the shattering of Old California, when the fault line ruptured and made the entire state a flooded island, and it was here that he was hoping to find answers. Gabriel needed to find this Seer and stop her from meeting the child of Cain. The archangel smiled when he thought back to eleven years ago, when he met the child of the world's first murderer. He had helped the mother cure the boy by giving her confidence and answering her prayers. Little did he know that he had played right into fate's plan. *Or was it Lucifer that was playing me?* Gabriel wondered, knowing that lately his fallen brother had been pulling strings.

Gabriel found a closed off portion of the sacred library and noticed that it had been plundered already. *No, not plundered, but taken,* he thought as the room wasn't tossed like it usually was during looting. *But by whom?* Frowning he closed his eyes and rubbed his temples, feeling a headache coming on. Gabriel was about to give up when he found a clue, lying on a dry shelf. It was an old shipping label, faded and worn, yet readable. *Someone didn't just break in and take everything,* he thought, *they packed it up neatly and shipped it!* Gabriel read the paper and smiled, Rand Industries. *Now where have I heard that name?* No matter, at least now he had somewhere to start.

Together at Last

He walked down Knob Hill and turned the corner, seeing the young man he was looking for. Natasha smiled as he felt destiny coming together after all these years and the spring in his step was genuine. He brushed his slick, blond hair back out of his brilliant hazel eyes as he sauntered up to the young man and stuck his hands in the pockets of his tailored, black, Armani suit. "You look like you're lost," Natasha said to the wayward young one as the child stood in front of a large window.

The young man turned, his brown hair and dark brown eyes reminding Natasha of the child's ancestor. The boy's own hands stuffed in his pockets, he turned to look at Natasha with skepticism, then shrugged. "My boyfriend, Simon wants us to get a pet together, to signify the next step in our relationship. I have no idea what to get for that." The young man turned back and looked at the different animals in the window of the pet store, indifferent to Natasha's steady gaze. "Who are you anyway? You an animal lover or something?"

"No, that's my sister. My name is Natasha and I have a thing for snakes, but that's neither here nor there at the moment," he said walking around the young man.

"What's your name," Natasha asked, knowing full well whom he was speaking to.

"Aleksandr," Alek said, smiling for the first time. "So, what do *you* recommend then?"

"Well, if you think about the different kinds of pets, it gets easier." The man who called himself Natasha took one hand out of his pocket and tapped on the glass, making a little puppy whip its head around and wag its tail. "Small apartment?"

"Yeah."

"Both of you work?"

"Um...yeah."

"So, a dog or cat seems too much work for either of you if it's the beginning of a relationship, right?" He smiled at how easy it was to lead young Aleksandr Cain down his path of reasoning. "Does Simon have allergies?"

"Not that I know of," Aleksandr said turning towards Natasha now, fully drawn into the conversation. "What's left? I don't want a bird."

"Heavens no! Birds are filthy creatures, though I do like wings..."

"So, what then?"

"Ah, well, you know it *is* spring right?" Natasha asked, smirking at Aleksandr. How like his family line to be guided this easily by impulse; cure or no cure. "Look at that fluffy little creature right there." Natasha pointed to the far corner where a fluffy white bunny sat, chewing on something.

"Hey, you have something there, mister," Alek said, placing both hands on the glass and looking in. "It's cute and quiet, sits in a cage...perfect!" The young man started to hurry into the store then stopped. "Hey, I really owe you one man."

"Oh, let's not go *that* far Alek...it's only a pet." The man whose name wasn't really Natasha smiled as Alek rushed away to buy his lover a bunny, the perfect gift for a springtime romance. Lucifer walked down the street, reflecting on what had brought him to this point after all these years. He was a fallen archangel and had been down among humanity since the first days of the garden, yet it wasn't until the humans broke the world that he started to truly care.

Lucifer had always hated humanity for replacing his role with Father; yet, he had seen them at their worst and he truly felt for them. That day, when they went too far, Lucifer had a vision of the future. He had seen two children, the young man he just talked to, and his lover Simon, falling in love and bringing the full light of heaven down upon them. He could only assume it was because of who they were...the blood of Cain and a seer of God. The vision had showed him how he could truly find his way back home, and though it didn't give him an exact blueprint of what to do, he knew that these two had to fall in love.

Lucifer had worked for decades to make sure these two boys lived and met each other, even going so far as to include his brothers and sisters on the game board, pieces to manipulate to his own ends. He was always good at that sort of thing. Imagine his surprise when fate itself had helped at certain points, even more than he could've foreseen.

Taking off one of his silver cufflinks and throwing it to the ground by the door for Alek to find, Lucifer spread his glorious white wings out before Aleksandr exited the store with his new pet, and flew away. *Well, one down, one to go,* he thought as he flew over the New Colorado cityscape, the fluffy clouds just out of his reach. Now he just had to let Alek go home to Simon Rand before his brothers realized what was happening. *And then I'll set the final pieces into motion...*

THE SEER'S GIFT

Simon Rand picked up the toaster and kicked another empty box to the side. He was almost done unpacking and then he could collapse on the couch and take a break. He couldn't believe he had moved in with his boyfriend so soon, yet it felt perfect. Simon wasn't your normal eighteen-year-old African-American young man. His eyes, like pools of liquid chocolate, could see the divine gifts of the world, glowing like beacons in the dark night. He had this ever since he was young, helping his father, David, pick out which religious artifacts were authentic. Simon sniffed back a tear, the memories creeping back in. His mother had died the year after his father had a heart attack and he had gone into foster care. He was adopted six months later by a friend of the family—a loving woman named Amanda Slone—and the two had formed such a bond that he had come to think of her as his second mother.

She, too, could see some things like he could, albeit not as much. Amanda helped him grow into the young man he was today, yet everything changed last year when she also died in a car accident and he had been thrown into a downward spiral of depression and darkness. That's when he met Aleksandr. Simon remembered his first encounter with the young man and being shocked at the name; the same name as an angel that had saved his family once over a decade ago as well as saved his foster mother when she was younger; It was all too coincidental.

Simon sighed and went back to unpacking, his boxes almost empty. Alek had been a ray of sunshine in his life, literally glowing at times. The young man had to have some sort of deep connection to the divine, yet Simon didn't care. He was a caring, handsome, thoughtful man, who just happened to love him for who he was. It wasn't until six months later that they had told each other the bizarre things that happened to them when they were younger. Simon had reluctantly told Alek that he was saved by an angel, thinking the guy would run out on him then and there, yet Alek only laughed.

Aleksandr then told him that he was born with a rare form of rage that almost killed him, but was saved by a stranger's blood at the last moment; a stranger that went out a four-story window and was never found. They seemed like they were destined for each other.

Still Simon had his doubts. They had moved to the rebuilt section of New Colorado, wanting the safety of a building rather than the forest like some people. It was nice, but he still needed to be sure Alek was the one. That was why he had sent Aleksandr out for a pet. He had told him it was to bring them closer together, but he had lied. In truth he wanted to see what he would choose for a pet. To Simon, choosing a pet was symbolic. If it was high maintenance, then it could spell trouble for the lovers trying to start a life together, too simple—like a stupid bird—and it would show that he didn't put enough thought into it. He knew it was kind of shallow, but it was something Amanda had taught him. To be picky with whom you gave your heart to. He sat down finally, just as the front door opened, the sound of the key pad chiming slightly announcing Aleksandr. "Alek, you're home!" Simon said, then stopped cold, standing up and shaking as he stared at the young man.

"Hey, Simon," Alek said, turning and bringing a cage out from behind his back. "Look what I have!" he said in a sing-song voice. He also stopped when he saw his love's face, his eyes wide with shock. "What?"

"Where did you get that?" Simon asked.

"The pet store? Is that a trick question?"

"No...that," Simon said pointing to Alek's other hand.

"Oh, this?" Aleksandr opened his hand and tossed the silver cuff-link on the counter. "I found it in the street when I left the store. I thought it looked pretty so I grabbed it for you. You like wearing those fancy suits so I figured it might go with one of them. Don't you like things like this?"

Simon was speechless, the cuff-link glowing like a mini sun all by itself. He had seen rare artifacts like Bibles and pieces of the original cross, and none of them had glowed like this. This was from something very close to God himself, yet seemed new compared to those other artifacts. *My Heavens, it's a sign*, he thought, falling to his knees. He had sent his love out on a test and he had passed in ways he couldn't have foreseen. Simon got to his feet and stumbled forward, kissing his lover deeply and pulling him close. They broke apart after a minute and looked into each other's eyes.

"I take it you like my choice?" Alek asked, holding up the cage.

Simon saw the white fluffy bunny and his heart melted, knowing that the choice was made with a thoughtful, caring heart. "Oh, Alek, it's perfect! I love you."

Too Late

The archangel Gabriel crumpled the papers in frustration and looked to the darkening sky. He had found the address on the paper, but Mary Rand had died years ago, their only son being adopted by a family friend. Worse still, he recognized the address from conversations with his brother, Azrael. The archangel of death had saved the Rand family years ago, here on Mercer Island retreat.

So, I help save Aleksandr Cain, and another archangel saves the family of his lover...oh Father what have you done? Gabriel walked back to the street, shaking his head. He would have to do research now and find out where the young Rand had gone before they bared their souls to each other. It wasn't just because they were both men—God was more open minded than most of the churches that represented him. No, the problem was the prophesy. He turned and looked up as a thunderous crash echoed throughout the sky, the black clouds gathering tight. A bolt of white-hot light lanced down to a spot in the distance and a great cry went up that only the archangel could hear. It was as if heaven was calling out to him. *I'm too late...*

Gabriel flew up, his gorgeous two-tone white/brown wings beating quickly, sending him aloft. He saw where the light struck and frowned. New Colorado was one of the most peaceful places in this new time. When humanity broke their world, some places were devastated: California, Arizona, Miami, and Nebraska to name a few. Some places, though, came out of it better than they were. New Colorado was one of them.

The massive city-state has high walls that surround a massive area from Boulder all the way to the national parks. Most people live in the forests, with very few preferring to live in the rebuilt city. It is a place of recreation and commerce, having the market on skiing, hiking, and tourism that only the New England City-States could compete with. If this was the site of the darkness that was coming, then his father was playing a cruel joke indeed.

"Ah, I see you've noticed the light show?" Lucifer asked, his white wings beating slowly in the air next to Gabriel.

"What have you done this time, Lucifer?" Gabriel asked calmly. He had never had a problem with his wayward brother, yet if he had caused this, there would be trouble.

"Natasha," Lucifer said calmly. "I go by Natasha now."

"Answer the question, brother."

"I didn't do much; just helped them pick out a pet."

"Don't lie to me."

"I don't lie, you know that." The fallen archangel hovered in the air, his wings beating silently. The two of them seemed like two sides of the same coin at that moment; both having blond hair and eye color that was similar, yet one in white and the other in black.

"Let me guess...you got them a snake."

"No, actually I convinced your ward, Aleksandr to buy a bunny."

"You jest."

"No. It's spring and the bunny symbolizes..."

"I know what a bunny symbolizes you filthy-minded beast." It dawned on him then, what Lucifer had done in truth. He had played matchmaker, starting this second coming of trouble to heaven.

Gabriel turned, his wrath boiling up from an unfamiliar place, yet his wayward brother was already gone. Gabriel sighed and flew off, letting his rage flow out of him. He was better at it then Michael ever was, letting go, that is. He tried to think of what he was going to do. If they had already bared their souls to each other, then it may be too late, yet if he could end it now.... Gabriel flew up, silently sending his plea to the heavens above. If he had Uriel send angels to end this charade of love before the darkness truly came, then maybe it could be averted after all. *I just pray that it can be averted...*

The Fall of Eve

THE MISSION

The sound of her black combat boots echoed across the parking lot as she stomped after her targets. They were headed towards the small beach on Grand Lake in New Colorado and she had to admit that it was a site to see, especially since she had only been on earth this time for about seven hours. The mountains reaching up in the distance and the cool water lapping quietly on the sand had this effect that she couldn't quite explain. It called to her on a level that she hadn't ever felt before. *No matter*, she thought. *I have to keep my focus.*

Evenal shook her head to clear it and tried to blend in, failing miserably. Along with those combat boots, she wore a long black dress and heavy black mascara, with obsidian jewelry adorning her wrists and neck; it made her stick out like a priest at a rave here at the beach. When she had been tasked with coming to earth once more, she had looked into what she wanted to look like. Evenal was drawn to the rebel look of the late-century gothic teenagers and it seemed to call to her rebellious side. Soon she had the complete look and descended from heaven ready to hunt. If she only knew how boring this mission would be, or where she was headed, she might've gone with something else; it was a waste of her style to go after these two kids here in the mountains. She had been following the two love birds for over an hour now, observing them and trying to figure out why she had been sent here to eradicate them.

One of them, the African American boy was somehow gifted, as he could see things that no one else could. To make sure of this, she had left things for him to notice—one of her feathers here, a scribble of Enochian there—and he had seen them both, his wide eyes and intense stare giving him away. The other boy seemed familiar somehow, but she wrote that off for now. She had seen a lot of people over the millennia, watching humanity from the Silver Realm of Heaven; it could just be that he looked like someone she had observed. Evenal was a hunter angel, a specific type of angel tasked by the archangel Uriel to eliminate certain things that needed to be erased; the 'things' were almost always people.

Now, here she was in all her splendor, and she had to follow these two boys. *This is such a waste of time and effort,* she thought as she walked behind them. In centuries past she had taken out entire towers, cities, and even erased kings and queens; now her task was this?

Her quarry sat down at a picnic table and took out food from the backpack they had been carrying. She stopped, sliding behind a parked truck, and frowned. They were just here to relax, not cause some type of uproar. Evenal had *never* doubted her mission before, doing so could mean the ultimate punishment to one of her kind-the fall. Yet, this time something felt off with her current assignment. *My mission is clear*, she thought as she steeled herself to carry out the inevitable.

She unfolded her glorious two-tone black/white colored wings and flew quietly towards them, pulling her slim sword made of light. All angels had wings that no one could see. They were kept discorporate behind them, almost inside of them. When released, humanity cannot see them unless the angel wishes them to. When Evenal glided closer, she could feel something coming off of them, like a wave of pure emotion. This only happened when the people were special, chosen by God somehow. That's when she felt what the emotion was and knew in her very core that this was *wrong;* it was pure love.

*I can't do this...*Evenal arched upwards toward the sky, racing to get back before it was too late. She started screaming silently in frustration as she felt the heat increase all around her. *No...please...it's wrong! Not this!* Yet it had already started the minute she disobeyed God's will; Evenal had fallen.

Devil's in the Details

The handsome man walked down the street looking at humanity and wondering, not for the first time, why he was really here. Not here as in Ruined Nebraska, but here on earth in general; nobody in their right mind came to Nebraska if they had a choice.

The entire state had gone up in flames when the world broke, some of the fires still burning and no one knew why. There were theories, of course, but with the world in chaos, no one really cared enough to find out. Now, most of the places that weren't on fire were desolate, nearly empty, rural towns and conglomerate villages just trying to survive. The land was scorched and barely workable, yet the survivors really had nowhere else to go.

The man called Natasha smiled as one man walked by, obviously sizing him up for some kind of theft or hit— Natasha knew that look by now. He brushed his slick blond hair back out of his hazel eyes as he sauntered through the desperate crowd, sticking his hands in the pockets of his tailored, Armani suit. He knew he was out of place, he always was, here on earth, yet somehow no one really seemed to notice overmuch. The people were just too despondent to care about outsiders. He turned the corner into an alley, knowing that the man following would see this as an opportunity too good to pass up.

"Alright mister, hands out of those pockets and give me that fat wallet." The sentence was punctuated by the rough jab of metal in Natasha's back.

"Oh, friend, you have no idea what you have gotten yourself into, yet I'm feeling pretty good this day," the man that was definitely not human said as he turned slowly to face the miscreant behind him. "I know you're probably just trying to feed your family, so I'll make you a deal. If you walk out of this alley right now, I will forget you ever existed and you can go about your life in peace." The man, who in reality was the fallen archangel Lucifer, smiled and made his eyes flash with a deep red to send his message a bit more clearly. He chuckled as his attacker both soiled himself and turned to flee at the same time.

"That was generous for someone who is supposed to be the devil." A lyrical voice said from behind him.

Lucifer turned and saw his brother, the archangel Gabriel, standing there with his own hands in his pockets, leaning against the brick building. "Are you still cross with me over those boys, brother?"

"No, *Natasha*," Gabriel started, using Lucifer's earthly name these days, "I am not. I have a plan in place to fix your meddling, do not worry."

"Ooohh, a plan. I'm excited to see that fail." Lucifer walked forward, and clapped his brother on the shoulder. "Yet, I think you're still cross with me about that bunny."

"I am not Michael. I can let things go," Gabriel said, turning and walking with his fallen brother as they exited the alley. "Yet, something still bothers me."

"Oh? What can I do to help with that?"

"Why you did all this in the first place?" Gabriel flipped his own long, dirty blond hair out of his emerald green eyes, and weaved through the crowd of people. Gabriel wore a white suit with white shoes, a vast contrast to the darkly dressed man next to him. "The kids and that business with the Blade of Enmon."

"All I can say is that this is supposed to get me absolved in our Father's eyes, brother, and I will do anything I can for that."

"You can't be serious?"

"I am, though I will admit I don't know exactly how that is going to happen. I only know that those two had to fall in love, the rest is obscured to even my foresight." All archangels had some kind of power aside from answering prayers. Azrael and Raphael could heal and even raise the dead, Gabriel could find anyone if there was a message to deliver, and Lucifer...he could see visions of the future. This foresight had helped him in the past, yet it was always vague. He had no idea what would happen now that he had put his plan in motion.

"And the Blade of Enmon?"

Lucifer laughed, knowing that Gabriel was talking about the very knife his brother, Michael, used to almost end his own life. "That was to get our brother home. He would've stopped those kids by killing them, and you know that Father takes the death of his own very personally. I wouldn't wish what happened to me on anyone, even Michael."

"Wait...his own?" Gabriel stopped short, two pedestrians slamming into him from behind at his abrupt stop. Despite his slight frame he never moved with the impact.

"What did you think a Seer was, dear brother?" Lucifer turned, but Gabriel was already gone, his gorgeous two-tone white/brown wings beating quickly into the sky. *Well, doesn't that just make my day.*

THE FALL

Falling from heaven's grace is different for every angel. The fall was both physical and spiritual at the same time and it wrecked the angel to their core. Evenal fell over the large lake, her wings aflame and the heat searing her lungs as she tried to scream her defiance. She desperately tried to steer sideways to lessen the impact, but her flaming wings were almost useless now. She did manage to aim closer to the shore and hit the water like a meteorite, skipping towards the sandy beach like a stone thrown from the hand of a child, water spraying over the tourists like a wave. Evenal landed with an impact that created a crater in the soft sand, one in which she lay smoldering. Thankfully, even burning, her wings kept people from seeing her, yet they wouldn't last forever. The flames licked at her skin and hair as, even soaking wet, her wings kept burning; such was the heat of the fires of God. Evenal lay there, weeping tears of flame, as her wings finally burned away into hot ash, the pain making her scream her sanity away. The ashes of her immortality falling around her and no one could see or hear her torment—well, almost no one.

Most of the people around her scattered from the invisible something that had hit the water, sprayed them all, then left a small crater in the beech; fear of the unknown struck terror into their fragile souls. Her wings gone, as were all of her clothes, Evenal lay there, naked and not burnt, in a large depression in the sand. Only two people ventured closer to see what happened.

"Are you alright?" The voice was soft and a little frightened.

"Alek, be careful she's...something else." This voice was a bit deeper.

Evenal knew that voice; it was the one that could see things. *It would be these two that would find me,* Evenal thought as she tried to stand up. She was completely naked, but otherwise unharmed for now, the loss of her wings notwithstanding. With the fall, things were unpredictable; her body could change at any moment or under any circumstance. The dark-skinned boy covered her in a huge towel as the other boy helped her out of the crater.

"My name is Aleksandr and this is Simon," The boy was dressed simply, but now she could tell that he was well muscled and with a frame meant for power. It was so familiar that she was kicking herself that she couldn't figure it out.

"What's your name?" Simon asked still staring at her with wide eyes.

Evenal contemplated it for a second and decided to go with an oldie but goodie, condensing her name into a classic. "Call me Eve."

"*What* are you?" Simon asked as they guided her towards the parking lot. People were running towards the crater now with cameras and even a small fire extinguisher, the small fires still licking the sand in places.

"Well now, *that* is an interesting question," Eve said, walking with them as they led her to their car. "I was an angel sent here to kill you, but I couldn't do it. Because I didn't follow that order, I fell."

"Like the devil did in the stories?" Simon asked curiously. He seemed like one of those kids that soaked up information and relaxed a bit more now that they were talking.

Before Evenal could answer, Aleksandr growled in frustration and punched his hip. "It's got to be because of that Adam guy." Simon laid a calming hand on his shoulder. It was touching to see.

"Who would that Adam guy be?" Evenal had this sinking feeling in the pit of her stomach, something she had never experienced being immortal. She didn't like this mortality thing already.

"His name is Adam Cain and he saved me years ago by giving my mother some blood to cure my affliction. I read that there was an explosion shortly afterwards, but my mother said someone named Michael was after him."

"Oh, for the love of Pete," Eve cursed as she shook her head. She knew now why she was sent to kill these two. It must be an affront to God to have these two in love; the descendant of Cain and a Seer of God. Cain's line was said to be cursed with the males dying from the rage inside of them, yet Alek seemed fine. *Cain saved him...what strange times are these that we dally with mortals.*

" So now you're...what, a normal girl?" Alek sounded doubtful and narrowed his eyes at his partner when Simon laughed outright at the statement.

"Normal? Far from it, you should see what I see Alek."

"Simon, be nice man, she's been through a lot."

"Sorry, Love." Simon smiled across at Alek and helped Eve climb into the back seat of the car. "Here, climb in and we can go find you some clothes."

"But you two could still be in danger?" Eve had no idea why they were still with her. She had told them she was there to kill them, and still they stayed with her. "Why are you helping me?"

"It's the right thing to do." It was a final answer that she had no rebuttal for and Alek's determined face now reminded her of Cain indeed.

Eve shuddered slightly. That jaw line, those eyes...it was frightening being in the presence of the first murderer's descendant; he was a bearer of the Mark of Cain, even if it were cleansed somehow. "Well, thank you, boys. Just get me some clothes and I'll see about finding some help from some others out here." In truth, she had no idea what she was going to do, but she couldn't stay here with them...that would make them even bigger targets. *And what am I going to do about Uriel? Surely he would send others to bring me back.* They drove off down the road as the sun set on Grand Lake, never seeing the winged angel set down lightly on the sand.

Flowers of God

Gabriel saw the fiery form falling from the sky, screaming in torment and knew that he had miscalculated. He had never even thought of the fact that you can't kill a Seer without angering Father. He had reacted like his brother Michael and now an angel was paying that price. He should never have involved Uriel and his hunters. Even worse was the fact that he could tell from the sound of her screams who it was.

"Oh, Evenal I'm so sorry," Gabriel said as he flew on, his brilliant two-tone white/brown wings bringing him there quickly. He could see the scorched sands from the sky and, as he alighted on the sands, he staggered slightly at what he saw. There in the crater of the ashes of burnt wings, was a ring of flowers. They had sprouted almost as he landed, growing impossibly quick and perfectly in bloom. They were lilies and it brought tears to the archangel's eyes to see them sprouting in the burnt and scorched sand like this. This was the second time he had received a message from Father in the past couple days; the first being a cryptic vision. This one however wasn't cryptic at all, but a direct message from above. Gabriel remembered the verse perfectly, as the messenger of God he could never forget anything that he read anyway. It was from Luke 12:27-28

Consider the lilies, how they grow: they neither toil nor spin; but I tell you, not even Solomon in all his glory clothed himself like one of these. But if God so clothes the grass in the field, which is alive today and tomorrow is thrown into the furnace, how much more will He clothe you? You men of little faith

Gabriel tore his gaze away from the flowers and searched his surroundings for the bodies of the children, yet saw nothing of the sort. Most of the humans were either fleeing in their cars or recording the event on their phones from a good distance, but he couldn't see any other signs of violence other than the crater. *So, she didn't kill him, yet she still fell? What am I missing?* Flowers blooming here, of all places, and from the ashes of a fallen angel on top of that, wasn't something you saw every millennium. That's when it hit him; Lucifer was right all along when he said this was meant to be. "He even said it was spring," Gabriel said to no one in particular as he turned and beat his glorious wings once more, taking flight. *I wonder if Lucifer knew that when he said it?*

Gabriel shrugged as he flew; it mattered not. Uriel, the archangel of knowledge, was in charge of the angels sent to erase threats. He wouldn't know of the significance of the message and had probably already sent another hunter angel after Evenal. Fallen angels weren't allowed to stay on earth; Lucifer was an exception to this rule and was the catalyst for the hunters to be created in the first place. They had failed in the past to bring the devil's followers back, so every new Fallen was hunted quickly before they found help. They would drag her back and recondition her into the fold once more. *Well, this time they will have to get through me as well.*

Hunted

PLANS CHANGE

He paced in front of the statue, seemingly oblivious to the stares of his underlings, his silver wings bristling with agitation. He blew a strand of light brown hair out of his face and glared at the statue with a critical look in his grey eyes. The statue, located in the Silver Realm of Heaven, was of Noah and was kept here to remind the hunter angels that some things were worth sacrificing for. His mission had failed, yet now he had a new problem to deal with. He was tasked by Father to bring back all fallen angels into the fold, if possible, and he had just lost his most dispassionate hunter. Evenal had fallen because of this failed mission, and he would see her back no matter the cost.

The archangel Uriel stopped suddenly, the clouds he was walking on puffing up at his abruptness. He sensed a presence coming that was stirring up the heavens and his hunters backed away at the look on his face. He saw things that others didn't, things that would happen if the right events were set in motion. "Welcome, Michael," Uriel said just as his older brother appeared before him, his golden hair falling over broad shoulders.

"Uriel, Gabriel says you have to stop now," Michael said, his brilliant white wings flexing outwards.

"I have done as requested and ceased the attacks upon the fated children, though I believe you are all wrong." The prophesy that Gabriel had told them about was dark and ominous, referring to two young men that could throw the heavens into dark times again. He had sent his best hunter, Evenal, to erase them—only to lose her, too. Now, it seems they couldn't be touched because one of them was one of Father's seer's.

"Uriel, why do I hear that you are still sending hunters?"

Uriel spun on his brother, anger flaring in his hard eyes. "Because my job hasn't changed, Michael, I bring the fallen back into the fold, no matter the cost."

"Like you've brought back Lilith, Belial, and the others?" Michael's voice, while stern, was softer than usual, almost caring.

"You know Nergal and Belial have no true forms anymore. They are special cases that have to be dealt with carefully." He walked away folding his arms behind his back. "As for the others, it has been too long and their transformations have truly made them unredeemable. Evenal, though, has just fallen and it is possible to bring her home, like Sephiral was decades ago."

"Prudence, my brother, remember that virtue when you send them against her. Gabriel means to help her and we do not want another war amongst brothers."

Uriel chuckled softly and hung his head. "What happened to you, Michael?" the archangel of knowledge asked quietly. "You've changed since you were down there amongst the rabble."

"I learned some things that I had forgotten, and since Father spoke—"

"And yet I have been in charge up here for millennia," Uriel interrupted, "...while you have been playing mortal and chasing those humans. Now you come back, all soft hearted and caring, and think to issue commands?"

"They are warnings, not commands, brother."

"They are the same thing coming from your mouth, *brother*. Now, begone and let me instruct my angels on their target." He turned, but Michael was already gone, causing whispers amongst his hunters. "Enough. You know your target and what she looks like. Find Evenal and bring her home at all costs." Uriel turned back to the statue of Noah and smiled. That was a simpler time to be sure and one he missed dearly.

With the Dawn

She stood on the porch and sipped a delightful mixture of dark bean and hot water, mesmerized at the coming dawn as it spilled over the quaint horse ranch. *How have I missed this over the centuries?* she thought as she took another pull off of her coffee. *Who knew humans could come up with something like this?* Evenal, now going by the name Eve, looked again at the rising sun, and wistfully thought of the life she now had to lead—a life on the run and in hiding.

"Morning, Eve." The tired voice of the old woman echoed across the open porch as she came out and shuffled into her rocking chair. "Sleep well?" Margaret Cain had one of those voices that just drew your attention no matter what you were doing. Not that it was a horrible sound, just a gravely tone that you needed to listen to for some reason.

"I did, indeed, Margaret, thank you." Eve smiled at the woman and couldn't help but laugh inside at the irony of her lineage. The old woman was a descendent of Cain, the first murderer, and here she was sheltering a fallen angel. *Oh, the irony.*

"Your skin seems to be doing better, dear."

Eve pulled the long-sleeved shirt down over her arms and turned back to the horizon. She had been an angel in Heaven sent to kill Margaret's grandson and his lover. When she couldn't do it, though, she fell from Grace, both figuratively and literally. When an angel fell from Grace, they actually lost their wings, their bodies sometimes melting away or deforming. Others changed completely, their bodies adapting, but they were the minority. She had impacted the ground hard, but seemed to walk away unscathed...until that night when the moon rose high in the night sky. Eve's skin started to flake high up on her arms and legs, creeping down past her knees and elbows but stopping there. The skin had hardened into some sort of scales, almost like a dragon, and had turned a deep black to match her raven hair. "Yeah, well, the skin cream Aleksandr gave me is helping," Eve lied. The two boys she was supposed to erase had brought her to their apartment to get some clothes, then they drove her here, to an isolated farm on the edge of New Colorado; they said it was a place where she could feel safe for a bit and figure out what to do. It was Aleksandr's grandmother's place and she always helped his friends, especially since he had a falling out with his mother.

"Well, that's good dear, now you make sure you go and feed Whinny and Albert this morning once you're done." Margaret didn't wait for an answer, just turned and sat down in a chair.

"Yes, Ma'am." Eve smiled and walked down the steps towards the barn, sipping her coffee again. Whinny and Albert were horses that had belonged to Margaret's husband. He had passed some years ago—prompting the woman to go back to her maiden name—but the old woman still kept up the horses that the love of her life had adored. Eve walked into the barn and immediately heard the horses react to her presence. She may not be an angel anymore, but she was far from human.

"It's just me, guys," Eve said quietly as she set her cup down on the bench just inside the door. She had been here for six days now and the equines had figured out that she wasn't a threat to them, even though she smelled different. Eve went about brushing the horses and feeding them, marveling at their beauty and power. Whinny was a gorgeous, white, mare and Albert was a brown stallion fit for a king in her eyes. She had never bothered with animals before, being singular in her purpose when told to come to earth and fix a problem. Now that she had the time to sit back and see certain things, she could totally see why Lucifer had never tried to come back home. *Not that he would've been able to, though,* she thought with a chuckle.

It took about two hours but she finally got her morning chores done, including cleaning out the stables. She sat back on a pile of hay with her cold coffee and smiled. It was a small price to pay for the old woman's hospitality. Eve was a mess, especially since she was dressed in baggy clothes that Margaret had found in her husband's old closet. The boys had saved her when she fell but all of her original clothes had burned off with her wings. She got up and walked back to the house but stopped at the door when the horses got agitated once more. She turned and frowned, wondering why they were annoyed with her presence so soon. "Usually, you guys are fine once you've seen and heard me...what did I do now?" The horses fretted nervously in their stalls, butting the doors, and kicking the back walls. It was more than usual and it suddenly dawned on her that this might not be for her. Dread coursed down her spine at the thought of what it could be and she closed her eyes. She readied herself mentally for the challenge ahead—she had been found...

Sacrifice

Kalian landed gently outside of the barn, folding his bland, brown wings and scouring the area for his target. "I could sense you from the sky, Evenal. Hiding is beneath you, so just come out and we can be on our way home." Kalian was not in the mood and wanted to be back in Heaven as fast as he could. He hated retrieval missions and would rather just erase targets and be done with it.

"I'm not going back, Kal," Eve said as she came out of the red structure.

"Well, that's a different look for you, sister," Kalian said, almost laughing at her appearance. She was dressed in baggy jeans and a flannel shirt that seemed two sizes too big for her. It seemed comical that she was taking a stand looking like this. "You've fallen, Evenal; you don't have much choice in the matter."

"I go by Eve now, and I can still take you, *little* Kal."

Kalian's blue eyes narrowed and he flushed in anger. He had always been the smallest angel, only standing four feet eleven inches. The other hunter angels always picked on him and pushed him around, yet he took it in stride. After all, they were all Father's children. "Eve, is it? It is ironic that you would choose the name of the traitor to the garden." He tied his light brown hair up in a pony tail and advanced cautiously.

Eve backed up into the barn, leading him after her and away from the house. It was a delaying tactic probably meant to spare the human that was helping hide her. "I don't think Father saw it that way, Kalian. After all, He let them go and create humanity just as He planned, right?" As Eve passed the stables of the horses, she released the latch with a quick flick of her wrist. She kept backing up as the beasts plowed out and ran interference for her.

Kalian saw the panicked animals and stopped, knowing that they could inflict some damage if they were to turn their full attention on him. He may be an angel, but the body he had could still be ruined which would send him home prematurely. Kalian watched her continue backward until she opened the rear doors to the large coral, giving the horses somewhere to go away from him. *A coral, how appropriate,* he thought as he laughed at her planning. *Now she is trapped just like the animals she has been grooming.* "Nowhere to go now, *Eve*," he sneered as he pulled his slim sword out and held it in steady hands. "I didn't want to use this, but you're giving me no choice."

The horses fled out of the open doors and ran for the far corner of the field, leaving Eve and Kalian to stare at each other. "Kal, you don't have to do this..."

"Do you want me to disobey and fall from Grace as well?" Kalian asked, as he advanced upon her. He never received an answer as they closed and lunged at each other. They were both well trained, having millennia to study war and styles. Kalian had his sword, but Eve had size and reach to her advantage. Every time he thought he had her, she got inside of his reach and he had to resort to close combat, blocking her attacks with his off hand and knees as she came at him like a savage. The two times he did get past her defenses, his sword clanged off of some sort of scales on her arms. Even though she had lost her grace, she could still fight. Kalian knew that he was in trouble unless he finished this quickly.

As an angel, Kalian still had superior speed and strength, yet, to his dismay, her skill surpassed everything he could muster. However, he was not without tricks. He deliberately left himself open and waited for her to strike. When she lashed out with a kick, knocking him back several feet, he recovered and lunged with his slim sword impossibly fast and put all his strength behind the blow. He knew that she would be off balance from the kick, but this would leave him vulnerable; it was a chance he was willing to take. Just when he could see an end to the fight, his strike hit a brown blur. It knocked him sideways with such force that he rolled twenty feet before he could right himself. He felt several things snap inside his chest and all he could hear was the whooshing of air and Evenal screaming.

Leaving Ruin Behind

Eve stroked Albert's head as the horse lay there, bleeding out. The slim sword had torn a huge gash in the animal's side and there was nothing she could do without her powers. She felt totally useless for the first time in her very long existence. Whinny was neighing fitfully in the distance and Eve could completely understand the feeling.

She had never felt this ache in her chest before and if these humans went through this for an animal, she could only imagine the weight of losing a loved one. She heard Kalian groan and roll to his knees and her eyes hardened as she stood and stalked towards him.

"It's over Eve, just come home..." Kalian started to say, and then he staggered back as his left shoulder exploded in gore as the deafening roar of a shotgun echoed across the ranch.

"Kill *my* animal will you, you son of a bitch!" Margaret screamed as she cocked the gun again and took aim.

Eve saw Kalian unfold his wings and knew that the old woman was doomed. "Margaret, look out!" she called, knowing the woman wouldn't be able to see her target anymore. She ran forward to stop the hunter angel but Margaret fired first, aiming in the general direction of where she last saw him, scoring a lucky graze on the angel's wing and spinning him around as he charged her. Eve was on him then, taking him down to the ground in a heap, punching and ramming his head into the dirt. In the end, she ripped the sword out of his hand, held it high in both hands, then brought it down with such force that it buried in his chest to the hilt. The blow sent him back to Heaven, his fading scream echoing in her ears as she tried to catch her breath. She knelt panting, exhausted ,and covered in blood and mud. *I killed one of our own,* she thought with deepening sadness. *Yet, I had no choice.* That was when she realized Margaret had been quiet...too quiet.

Eve turned to the old woman who sat there clutching her chest in the dirt, smiling at the sky, her face a mask of pain and fear. "Margaret!" Eve called out and scrambled to her side. "Hold on. I'll call Aleksandr and Simon; they'll know what to do." Eve fumbled for the phone they had given her, but she wasn't good with it yet and kept shutting it off.

The old woman's face cleared then, as if she had seen something that even Eve couldn't see. "It's...it's fine dear, I'll be with my love soon and...and," with that Margaret grimaced and collapsed, her eyes softening as the breath went out of her quietly; her heart had stopped.

Eve sat there for awhile and cried softly until something nudged her from behind. It was Whinny. As Eve stood, the horse ran off once more, running around the boundary of the fence that kept her in. Eve looked around at the coral as the horse ran free...free yet contained for her own safety. *Just like humanity*, she thought. *And I have to learn the boundaries of that fence I have to live in now as well.*

Two hours later Eve was walking down the empty road, having left a message on the fridge for Alek and Simon about their poor grandmother. She had finally called them and told them to hurry, but didn't want to be there when they arrived; she had placed enough people in danger as it was. It was going to be a long walk to the city, but she now had a plan in mind, at least. She needed to find someone—someone like her maybe—and try to blend in.

First, though, she needed a shower and some clothes that fit. *And a good cup of coffee.*

Farewells

He alighted silently as the boys cried on the porch, his gorgeous two-tone white/brown wings rustling as he stood. The archangel Gabriel had sensed the fight but it took him too long to get here. His long, dirty blond hair was covering his emerald green eyes as a tear fell down his own face. He had asked his brother Michael silently about Margaret and confirmed that she was indeed with her husband in Heaven. He had feared that helping to kill an angel had ruined her chances, but it seems that even Father was paying attention to the circumstances lately, even though some others had said that he had been absent of late.

"Whoever you are, thank you for coming," Simon said, the dark-skinned young man looking in his direction with unfocused eyes.

Gabriel sighed, forgetting that Simon Rand was a Seer of God and could sense things like him, even with his wings out. A sound caught his attention then and he flew off in the direction of the barn. He landed in the field as the white mare ran along the boundary of the fence, a familiar face watching the gorgeous animal. "Ariel, I'm surprised to see you here," Gabriel said as he saw the archangel of nature sitting on the fence. She ran her fingers through her long brown hair, strands the color of the very earth they walked upon. She wore a green shawl and faded jeans, with deep brown wings fanned out behind her.

"I felt that death more keenly than any other on this earth, Gabriel," she said, a deep sadness in her voice. "I think that stallion sacrificed himself for something greater than either of us can comprehend, though Raphael would understand it; it was love."

Gabriel walked over and hugged his sister, knowing that she felt these deaths keenly. "I think you may well understand that feeling as well, dear sister," Gabriel said with a knowing look. Word had spread among them that Cain and Ariel had taken to being close lately—really close.

"You don't want to listen to those rumors," Ariel said, yet blushed anyway. "So, what are you going to do now?" she asked, changing the subject.

"I don't know. I think it's time I asked our fallen brother for help."

"Still protecting Evenal?"

"You've heard?"

"Everyone has heard."

"Well then. I guess it really is time to get some help." Gabriel smiled as he flew off, knowing that this would divide Heaven even further; yet, in his heart he knew that he was right. *Hang on Eve, help is coming.*

In the Grip of Evil

OPPORTUNITY SEIZED

He limped around his abode and smiled, his mismatched eyes—one blue and one hazel—dancing with sadistic glee. Marcus Brant looked like he was sixty, yet he was a lot older than that. The real Marcus had been drained away many years prior to make way for the being using the body now. "You're certain it was an angel that fell?" he asked the nervous man standing in the doorway. His followers were a skittish bunch, probably due to the harsh beatings he doled out for failure. Klein was no different, but he, at least, had the spine to tell him the truth.

"Our sources say that something impacted near the lake in New Colorado and walked away with help eight months ago." Klein looked around at the room and swallowed, visibly shaken.

"You still don't believe in all of this do you?" The thing that wasn't really Marcus asked sardonically. His followers—cult really—had been worshiping him for centuries but it wasn't until he took physical form as Marcus that they really knew that he was real. Sadly, by then it was too late-as humanity choose right then to break their toy. Marcus barely survived the ordeal, and had a permanent limp to show for it. Still, with the power coursing through him, a little limp never slowed him down much.

His real name was Belial, himself a fallen angel at the time of the rebellion in Heaven. He had leapt after Lucifer when the archangel was thrown down, and had paid for his loyalty in pain and suffering. His glorious two-tone silver/copper wings had burned away, yet the flames didn't stop there. The writhing licks of fire consumed his body and almost his very soul as he fell, leaving him an incorporeal thing of wandering misery. From then on, he found that he could possess people and control other people's carnal desires. He went through the world inhabiting bodies, but they would rot quickly, a black disease that consumed the host within a year or so. The one thing he had found was that if the host had Heterochromia—mismatched eyes like this one—then the body could contain the spirit of the fallen angel. Sadly though, he was still aging, albeit slowly, and this body would eventually die leaving him formless once more. That was why he needed that fallen angel's body. Something like that, designed to house a spirit that strong, could last forever.

"Well, that is...I...." Klein sighed and closed his eyes, then turned around. "It's just that angels never seemed real to me, sir. My life was one of loss and fear and no matter how many times I prayed to God, things never got better."

"Well, He doesn't make things *better,* Klein, He has abandoned you all." Belial knew that from personal experience. His father had let him burn away to almost nothing, ignoring his cries and begging. As he screamed, his tears had mixed with the bits of ash and formed a set of small horns. He used these horns to gain his cult following over the centuries, leaving them apart and having them hunt for them. They had treated them like holy relics and hung behind him on the wall as they spoke. "But that matters not; in time you will come to know that this is real, regardless of your beliefs. For now, I want you all to work on tracking this fallen angel and bringing her to me. Her body won't age like this one; and in hers, I could truly live forever." Marcus watched Klein walk out quickly, eager to be gone from the presence of his lord.

Belial smiled and sat down behind his desk, pleased that his information network had survived the calamity that the humans brought upon themselves. The ruins of Chicago were his now, and though they lived in squalor, there was no one to impede his workings here in the rubble of the Windy City. When the calamity struck, the entire city of Chicago had fallen down at once, its massive buildings mostly piles of rubble now. The streets were jammed with chunks of stone or overturned cars and people lived in hovels and shelters made from the debris. He didn't mind it though...he had seen worse. The old stories called him a demon, and the name never fit so well to him as right now. *Yes, and I can't wait to see which one of my brothers or sisters have fallen from grace,* he thought, sitting back, and lighting a cigar.

Chained

She ducked down the alley and ran on, trying to keep her breathing under control. Eve had been running for a long time now and she just couldn't shake these guys in robes. Every time she thought she had lost them, they turned up once more on her tail. *At least they're not hunter angels,* she thought as she turned down another alleyway.

She kicked refuse out of her path as she clambered up a dumpster and leapt for the fire escape ladder, dragging it down and climbing as fast as she could.

Eve, or Evenal, as she was known among the angels, had fallen from His grace and was now trying to make her way among the humans. It was hard enough hiding from the ones sent to drag her back to heaven, but now these guys were after her as well. *And I thought angels were relentless,* she thought as her arms burned from the exertion. *These guys won't quit.* She had crippled at least three of the thugs in robes the third time they jumped her and still they didn't take the hint. Scrambling onto the roof, Eve rested a second and brushed the raven hair out of her face, seeking her next move. Although she seemed human with a casual glance, further scrutiny would reveal that she was indeed something more.

When she had fallen and her wings burned away, Eve's skin had started to flake high up on her arms and legs, creeping down past her knees and elbows but stopping there, the skin hardening into some sort of scales, almost like a dragon, and turning a deep black to match her raven hair. Because of this she could take a good deal of punishment and dish it out as well, almost like she was wearing armor. *Not going to help me if they get me cornered with the numbers they have.* Her thoughts spun as she started running again, leaping onto another roof below the one she was on. She hit hard and rolled, exhaustion finally catching up to her. She stood on shaky legs and turned, coming face to face with three more men in dark robes.

"Our master wants to have a word with you," one of the men said, stepping forward hesitantly. He motioned for the other two to fan out around her and lowered his hood, revealing a handsome young man with blond hair and brown eyes. "If you come quietly then we don't have to hurt you." He said the words, but the tremble in his voice betrayed his conviction. He was afraid of her

"Even this tired, I could still rip the three of you apart; you realize that, don't you?" Eve asked, and then realization crept up her spine. They had no intention of attacking her...they were a diversion. She spun as the other two moved to her sides and saw five more men with a large metal net. They were getting ready to toss it at her; the heavy weights on the side told her that if it hit, she was in trouble. She rolled to the side, but one of the men flanking her got in the way and the heavy net came crashing down on both of them.

Even though she was stronger than normal, the net dragged her down in a heap with the guy next to her. Eve thought fast and rolled the man on top of her as the other men started kicking, their booted feet crashing down. While they were kicking the life out of their friend, Eve got her hand under one of the weights and lifted the net to slip under.

'Look out!" the blond guy cried out, backing away in terror. "She's getting free."

Eve got both shoulders out and was about to lunge when the net tightened around her head and pulled her back, the heavy line choking her. The men piled on her now, even as she grabbed one and tossed him towards the edge of the roof, sending him tumbling over. Her arms and legs were taking the beating well, but she was running out of air. Soon the darkness crept in and enveloped her.

The Search

He drove his sports car down the ruined street at speeds that most people would blanch at, taking corners with precision timing and squealing tires. He dodged pieces of building and overturned cars as he sped down the middle of the road, too wrapped up in thought to enjoy the challenge. The man called Natasha frowned and looked at the abandoned cars and refuse that lined the road as he flew through it all. Of all the cities he had visited since humanity decided to break their world, the ruins of Chicago were not in his top ten; not even top twenty. He shook his head again and smiled at why he was here though; who ever would've thought his family would ask him for help.

His brother Gabriel had asked him to help protect the fallen angel, Eve, from the hunter angels sent to drag her back to Heaven, and had done so with humble politeness. Natasha had jumped at the chance on general principles—anything to pour salt into that old wound and irritate Father and he was in. The only problem was that one of his old acquaintances had grabbed Eve first...and Belial was no angel—not anymore. He had tried to keep tabs on some of the angels that fell with him all those eons ago—Lilith and Asmodeus were always fun to party with— but Belial was one that he just couldn't deal with. The spirit that was Belial was angry and had never forgiven neither Father nor Lucifer for his state.

Natasha came out of his reflection in a rush as two men blocked the road ahead, slamming on his brakes and spinning the wheel. His car came to a stop sideways and he looked at the robed figures with a smile that didn't quite touch his eyes. "Oh, you really do *not* know who you are dealing with gentlemen," Natasha said as he grinned, brushing his slick blond hair back out of his eyes. His Armani suit, now with only one silver cuff link, made him seem as out of place in the ruined city as a priest in a brothel.

"We know exactly who you are, Lucifer, and we are here to ask you to turn around in the name of our Lord, Belial." If the man speaking had anything else to say, it was lost in a gulp as Natasha barked laughter.

"Our Lord," Natasha snickered. "You say that name, yet you don't really believe it; I can tell," Natasha said getting out of his car and leaning on it, examining his fingernails as if bored. Natasha wasn't sure how Belial knew he was coming and that bothered him more than a little. "Let me guess...you were expecting horns and a tail? Maybe a red skinned devil?" As Lucifer said this he stood straighter and dropped his arms to his side. Letting his eyes channel the power within him, they flared a deep red, changing the atmosphere to one of imminent danger. It was one of the things he used often when dealing with mortals; especially the dregs of humanity. It drew out their deepest fears and laid them bare to him. This, paired with his power of foresight, usually got him out of most altercations without violence; not that he was against fighting, but he preferred to be subtle, unlike some of his brothers.

"You...you can't scare us. Our Lord f...fell with you and he is powerful." One of the men was actively backing away making the sign of the cross—of all things—while this one idiot stood his ground foolishly and tried to puff out his chest.

Lucifer narrowed his eyes and lost what little humor he still had. "First of all, mortal, I did not fall. I was *pushed!*" He screamed so loud that dust fell from the nearby buildings. He surged forward, grabbing the front of the man's robe in his fist. Natasha lifted him off of the ground effortlessly, his anger only flaring his eyes brighter. "And secondly," he said, calming down a touch, "your *Lord* is only a ghost in this world, jumping from body to body, never having his own...that is not power; it is desperation." Natasha threw the man he was holding backwards into his car, denting the back panel with the impact; the man never moved as he slid to the ground. "Now look what you made me do...that won't buff out you know." Natasha dropped his mortal ruse and turned his gaze upon the remaining man that was slinking away. "Now, if you take me to your wretched hideout, I may not hurt you." Lucifer waved the second man towards his car, kicked the limp body of the first man out of the way, and opened the passenger side door like a gentleman going to the ball. *Looks like it's time to call Gabriel and let him know that I found his pet*, Lucifer thought as he drove away with his new guide. *It can be a family reunion.*

Fateful Rescue

Eve came to slowly, her thoughts swirling in a mire of confusion. She went to run her hands through her hair and looked down in shock as she couldn't move. Her wrists were restrained by thick silver manacles which in turn were attached to large silver chains anchored to the floor by a metal plate. She looked at her surroundings and realized she was in some sort of basement. The musty, damp air reeked of filth and refuse. There were no windows and only one door, which sat as a silent judge to her incompetence. *I can't believe they got the drop on me,* she thought as she tested the strength of her restraints. Even being stronger than most humans didn't help her as the chains held firm.

She was a prisoner for some sort of cult and she wasn't even sure which one that was.

Being held like this drew attention to the freedom she had, albeit fleeting, on the run since she had fallen from grace. It wasn't an ideal life, yet for the first time in her existence she was beholden to no one. As a hunter angel in Heaven, she had answered to Uriel, and of course, to Father; they all had. Now, here on earth, she was free-and she had found that she was enjoying that newfound life more than she had thought possible. Even the sadness she had experienced here on earth—like the death of Margaret—had added to her new life in ways she would keep forever. Now that this cult had her, it just reinforced the need to escape these bonds. *Yes, but which cult is this?* she asked herself looking around once more to see if she could spot anything. The men had been wearing dark robes with some sort of sigil emblazoned on them, but one she didn't recognize. She was knowledgeable about most religious cults; after all, she used to be the one that came down to erase those that went too far. Yet, this one eluded her. She tried to get her feet underneath her to stand, but the chains that had her bound didn't have enough give to let her.

"Not very comfortable, is it?" a muffled voice asked from the door. The sound of keys jingling and locks turning announced her visitor before the door swung open. He seemed old, maybe in his sixties, with a limp, and beautiful mismatched colored eyes. The man closed the door behind him and pocketed the keys, turning towards her with a slight smile. "My name is Marcus, or at least that's what I go by nowadays."

"Oh, crap. Was I supposed to care?" Eve asked, with dripping sarcasm. "Wait, start over, I'm sorry. This time I'll be ready." She feigned attention and opened her eyes wide as if really enthused.

"You angels are all the same, sarcasm to mask your impotence."

"Fallen angel, actually," Eve corrected.

"Oh, I am acutely aware of that, sister; you see, you are exactly what I need." The man named Marcus focused on her with an intensity as he stood there, that slight smile spreading as she felt his power wash over her.

Eve could feel her fear and trepidation growing, being stretched like a rubber band. He was using her emotions against her, making her feel things that she had buried down deep. Only one being she knew of could do that, yet he had been dormant for decades. "Belial...what do you need me for?" she asked as she tried to fight off the feelings slowly overwhelming her. She had nothing to fight this with and if she didn't figure out something soon, she was in trouble.

"Well, for one, I need that body," Marcus said as he walked forward with a confidence that shouted victory despite the limp. "You see, I can inhabit these humans, but they age, wither, and die. Even this body, whose eyes prevent the rot, can still get damaged and age. As an immortal fallen angel, your body will allow me to live forever as a young, hale woman."

"You would look good like that too, old friend, yet I can't let you do that," A seductive voice said from behind the old man.

Eve looked at the man standing there and was immediately drawn to his blond hair, handsome face, and beautiful eyes. He had a stance that shouted confidence and charm, as well as an aura of command. "Oh look, Belial, my savior has arrived," she said with effort.

Belial spun on the unwanted intruder. "How did you find me?" Belial howled as the newcomer's eyes flared red. Belial turned the full force of his power at the newcomer-to no avail.

"Oh, come now, friend, you know that doesn't work on archangels" The handsome man said dangerously as he narrowed those eyes. "And a little birdie named Nergal told me where to find you-and who you had. It seems he is a little jealous of your body."

"Wow, nobody likes you, do they?" Eve asked sarcastically.

Belial backhanded, her then turned back towards his guest. "You can't have her, Lucifer, she is mine," the fallen angel said standing his ground. "I hold sway in this city."

"In case you've forgotten who I am, old friend, let me remind you." Lucifer circled and his stance immediately screamed violence, the atmosphere of the room changing in a heartbeat. Gone was the charmer, now there was only a warrior.

"Lucifer?" Eve was speechless. She had of course known of the fallen archangel, but hadn't seen him since that fateful day when Michael had thrown him down. *And to think, I almost joined him back then*, she thought as she watched the standoff. She was so intent on the meeting of the two fallen ones that she was caught off guard by hands on her shoulders.

"Hold still, Eve," a voice whispered in her ear as the chains snapped quietly. Strong hands held her and helped her stand as Lucifer surged forward and slammed the man called Marcus into the wall with such force that plaster fell around them both. The older man screamed as bones snapped and he tried to kick at Lucifer, but the fallen angel was already behind him again.

"Too slow, old man," Lucifer quipped, shoving the man face first into another wall.

Eve lost sight of the confrontation as she was ushered out of the room. She was pushed down a hallway and out through a hole in the wall, its crumbling cement floor riddled with the bodies of robed cultists. She turned her head and beheld the face of Gabriel, his blond hair and green eyes an eerie similarity to the devil she just saw.

"Odd kind of rescue party, huh?" Gabriel asked as he discarded the large bolt cutters among the fallen bodies. Then he grabbed her around the waist and they were flying, his wings spreading out as they cleared the building.

Cleaning Up

Lucifer, or Natasha, as he liked to go by nowadays, dusted off his suit with a look of disgust. He abhorred violence, yet this time it was called for. *More than called for*, he thought as he stood over the defeated body of Marcus Brant. When he had seen the girl that his old friend was ready to sacrifice, something awoke inside of him. It was like he was seeing the sun for the first time-the feeling he actually had those many millennia ago when he had stood with Father in the very beginning, watching the light of the world. When Belial backhanded her, Lucifer couldn't contain his rage, lashing out with his fists when he usually never did that. Now that she had been led away by Gabriel, and the cult disposed of, he couldn't get her face out of his mind.

"You weren't supposed to hit the face," a voice said from the shadows.

"Sorry, old friend, I got carried away. I think it will still work though," Natasha said bowing slightly.

A translucent mist glided towards the fallen body of Marcus Brant and merged with it slowly. The body stiffened and sat up, groaning in pain. "I can't believe Belial fled a perfectly good body," Nergal said as he moved the limbs tentatively.

"Well, he was being beaten within an inch of his life, so he figured he would quit while he had a head."

"You always think you're funny."

"I think I'm adorable." Natasha smiled at his own joke and shook hands with the body that was Nergal. "Is the body salvageable?"

"Yes, mostly. A few broken bones but I can work with that. The face is damaged, though, so I'll have to get a new one."

"We're even now?" Natasha hated owing anyone, but this one was a big favor. Snitching wasn't big on Nergal's to do list, but he needed a body.

"Yes, Lucifer. We're even. Don't worry; I'll lay low for awhile. Maybe check out Nebraska." Nergal bowed slightly and took his leave.

"Lord?" a tentative voice called from the open door.

"Oh, yes, I forgot. I let you live." Natasha turned and beckoned the man in. "And please call me Natasha."

"Truly?"

"Yes. Why do you ask?"

"Well, it's just...that it...is really a girl's name." The young man winced as if he was doomed for saying so, but was greeted with only laughter.

"Oh, I know that, but I found a book, years back that alluded to spelling it backward and it just resonated with me... never mind, I'm rambling." Lucifer walked out the door, waving for his new lackey to follow. "Now this cult, I assume you call yourselves a cult?"

"Yes lor...I mean Natasha."

"Good. I need you to find me that girl again. This time, though, do not attack her; just give her a message from me."

"What message is that?"

"That I look forward to meeting her again now that she has her freedom back." Natasha turned to watch the sun setting slowly as they walked out of the building. It wasn't the same, but it would do for now.

Taking a Breath

IF YOU WANT SOMETHING DONE RIGHT

He scowled and sent his hunters flying away. Uriel was having a very bad time and he was just not in the mood for more reports on how they couldn't do what he wanted them to do. The Archangel of Knowledge turned and thought of the green pastures near the river Kyrial, transporting himself there with but a thought; he needed a break from his surroundings and this place, in the pastures of Heaven, settled him when he was upset. Uriel unfolded his silver wings and blew a strand of light brown hair out of his face and surveyed the clam waters with his deep grey eyes. He sat down and dangled his feet in the cool waters of the river, watching his reflection blur in the ripples. It had all gone wrong so quickly.

Uriel had been tasked by Father to bring all fallen angels back into the fold, yet Evenal had evaded all his attempts. It didn't help that his brothers were against him, but still it shouldn't have been that hard to grab one fallen angel. Oh sure, there were others that had stayed hidden after all these millennia: Nergal and Belial had lost their physical form so they were hard to capture; Mephistopheles, Asmodeus, and Lilith were just too powerful after all these eons, so they were considered out of the running, but he had brought home everyone else-except now.

"Enjoying the calm, reflective waters, brother?" a deep voice asked appearing beside him in a blink.

"Must you bother me, Michael?" Uriel asked, not bothering to look up at the archangel. He knew that condescending voice anywhere.

"Just wanted to see how it has been going lately."

Uriel turned then, anger shadowing his eyes. "You know very well how it has been going. Our brother is conspiring with Lucifer to keep that fallen angel hidden from me." He saw the blond angel's smile fade and knew he had hit it perfectly. "Yes, you forget, brother, I can see things sometimes and how they will play out." Uriel stood in a flash and spread his silver wings out fully, catching the rays of sun as they shown down through the blue sky. "Do you know that Belial had her? That formless demon almost had an angel's body to possess because they had kept her from my hunters."

"I did hear that, yes. I'm sorry, Uriel, but we all think she should stay free." Michael unfurled his bright white wings and locked his blue eyes with his brother's as he crossed his arms over his barrel chest. "Father has something important for her to do and we can't intervene."

"Watch me."

"You would defy Father just like your fallen brother?"

"*Do not compare me to him!*" Uriel screamed before turning and realizing he was alone. He stormed off, taking three steps, and then disappearing in a blink to end up in a great hall of marble columns. In all of Heaven, this is where he came to decide the important things in his very long life. It was the Hall of Learning and held all of the scrolls and books collected over the eons that had been penned by the holiest of men. Multitudes of scriptures and Bibles lay on wooden tables as well as ancient parchments, penned in various languages and styles. *If my hunters can't seem to get the job done, then I will go there myself and bring her home,* he thought as he sat and started reading one very ancient-looking book. *But first, let me read up on some others that may be of assistance while I'm down there.*

BREATHE

She blinked her eyes at the bright sunlight as she sat up on the park bench. People walked by with their dogs on leashes and shot disapproving looks towards her as she woke up. *Not where I pictured myself at all,* she thought as she stretched her arms out. She saw the black scales on her arms and thought better of it, then buried them once more under the newspapers that lay over her like a blanket. Eve had been on the run for a long couple of months and, after almost losing her existence to the fallen angel Belial and his demon cult, she was supposed to be taking it easy. Eve—or Evenal as she was known before falling from heavens grace—had been rescued by none other than the archangel Gabriel and the original fallen one, Lucifer. *Still can't wrap my head around those two working together.* Her thoughts amused her, though, remembering the devil's charm and wit as he saved her from the formless one. He fought for her and she didn't quite understand why that made her feel all tingly inside.

Eve shook her head and stood up, letting the newspapers fall to the ground, her trustworthy blankets for the night whisked away in the morning breeze. Gabriel had brought her to a motel room in The Virginia Council States to recuperate and rest, but she felt trapped and needed to get away. She left when he stepped out for a minute and ran on through the night, eventually ending up here in this park. She had lain down to rest when sleep had taken her. *Who covered me up though?*

"Get plenty of sleep missus?"

Eve turned sharply and fell into a defensive stance while raising her hands, open palm for deflection. When she was an angel, she was one of the best hunters they had; she was an expert in almost all of the fighting styles throughout the millennia. "Who are you?" she asked, backing up slowly while keeping her guard. The man seemed harmless, dressed in multiple layers, and reeking of wine and urine; yet, you never knew. The man had long, brown hair and no shoes on his feet. Yet his blue eyes seemed clear and focused. He had to be at least in his forties.

"Me? Oh, you can call me Jobe." He held out his olive skinned hand and noticed that it was filthy, so he pulled it back and spit on it, rubbed it on his dirty pants, then offered it again.

Eve rolled her eyes and took the hand in good faith, relaxing her posture a little as she scanned the park for anyone else watching them. Getting captured by a demon cult had done wonders for her paranoia. "I'm Eve. Am I to take it you are the one who watched over me last night?"

"Ha, nice name," the man said with a chuckle, then looked off into the sky.

"So, was it you?"

"Was it me what?"

"Was it you that watched over me?"

"Heh, you could say that, yes. I like watching over people who need it." He scratched his side and then turned to her and whispered. "Plus, I've been doing it a *very* long time."

"I just bet you have," she said, knowing full well that she was at least ten times his age. Still, the man had a good heart and she smiled at his kindness. In all her years as an angel, she had never seen this side of humanity, and it was sad that it took her falling to glimpse her Father's works up close. *This must be why some of the archangels came down to be amongst them after the calamity, to see them up-close.* "Well, thank you very much, Jobe, but I have to be going now."

"Well, I reckon that you might want to take a couple days and relax. You seem stressed out, if you don't mind me sayin' so."

"If it was only that easy to relax." Eve could hear an accent, yet she couldn't place it.

"That's just it, missus, it can be." Jobe leaned in again, his rancid breath wafting towards her with every syllable. "You see, I have a little place that no one knows about just down there." He pointed to the vast shrubs bordering the fountain and smiled.

"I don't want to put you out or anything," Eve said, knowing that if they came for her he might be caught in the crossfire. *Just like Margaret,* she thought, remembering the old woman who had sheltered her when she first fell.

"Missus, sometimes you just need to sit and breathe." Jobe said as he grabbed her hand and led her towards the bushes. "And God above knows it doesn't seem like you've done that too often the last couple days."

Dark Dealings

Uriel felt the hard gravel under his feet keenly as he stood in the falling rain. His brown hair fell into his eyes and the water dripped down his face. This was not what he had anticipated when he chose to come down among the humans. Now, he found himself in a dark alley—in the rebuilt city of Cairo, Egypt—waiting for a door man to get whom he needed. The small panel slid open and a rough face greeted him.

"What."

"I have it on good authority that you are the man to get things done." Uriel said wiping the rain out of his face.

"Get lost, asshole. I don't do pity work." The man started to slam the panel closed but stopped when Uriel called him by name.

"Now, Shimshon, don't be like that." Uriel waited as the door slowly opened and the massive frame of the big man filled the doorway.

"My name is Sampson and who, the fuck, are you?"

Uriel let his wings unfurl then willed the man known as Samson to see them before putting them away. "My name is Uriel and you could say that I'm a very good friend from the old neighborhood."

"Crap. Come in before anyone sees you." Samson led him down a flight of stairs to a huge room. Samson was best known for his long hair, which was braided down his back. The thick, brown locks were brimming with power from an old curse. He had olive skin and the eyes of a killer. Sunday school skipped over his murders when they talked about the Bible. Samson had been a force of violence in the old days. He once killed over one thousand Palestinians with a piece of bone.

"Nice place you have here, Samson." There were weapons everywhere, both archaic and modern, with tapestries of the legendary warrior adorning every wall. Uriel stopped in the center of the room as Samson turned and sat down, eyeing him with suspicion.

"Speak your mind, angel, and be quick. I have no use for heavenly messengers these days," Samson growled.

"It's archangel, actually, and I am here to acquire your services." Uriel walked forward slowly, ready for the man to launch into an attack at any moment. If the stories were true, this man was unpredictable at best.

"What service could I possibly help an archangel with?"

Uriel smiled. "I have a person that I need taken and she has eluded capture from every hunter I have sent. You have the uncanny knack of never failing, so, I am here to hire you."

"Taken? Is Heaven kidnapping people now?" Samson asked with a smile that never touched his cold eyes.

Uriel shuddered at that smile. "No, Samson, we're not. She was an angel but she fell from grace. I have been commanded to bring all such failures back home."

The big man stood in one movement and walked to the side wall, dragging his fingers over a row of spears. "You know, when the Philistine leaders assembled in that temple for their sacrifice to Dagon, I thought it was over. The temple was so crowded that people were even climbing onto the roof to watch—and all the rulers of the entire government of Philistia had gathered as well." Samson chuckled as he recounted the tale and hefted a spear off the wall with rough hands. "They had no idea that while I was imprisoned my hair had begun to grow again. I prayed and then Michael came, in all his glory. No one could see him except me and he touched my hair, causing it to grow longer in seconds. I could feel the power flow into me and I pulled the supporting pillars down, causing the temple to collapse and killing all the people inside."

"Yet, you survived..."

"Yeah, my family dragged me out of the rubble, my wounds already healing. When I stood up, they screamed and fled, telling everyone I was dead. They "buried" me next to my father." Samson turned with one fluid motion and let the spear fly, the heavy instrument of death slamming into the opposite wall with such force that the walls shook. Four feet of it went through the wall before the weapon stopped.

"You prayed for the strength to bring down your enemies," Uriel said, remembering that day when Michael flew down to that temple. Dagon had been dealt with after that, yet Michael was a bit theatrical in those days and had given the warrior immortality as long as his hair was long.

"Right. My fault. Since I was now an abomination, everyone was an enemy. Typical angelic rhetoric." Samson went over and ripped the spear out of the wall with barely any effort. The man had the strength of at least ten men. "Did you know I've tried even cutting this hair once? To see if I would finally die?""

"Yet, you're still here," Uriel said carefully. He wasn't sure where this line of conversation was going.

"Yes, I am. It didn't work. Oh, I cut myself after that and I seemed mortal, but my hair grew faster than I could age. I can be killed, but it would take someone of immense skill and strength to do it." After a long silence, Samson walked over and put away the spear. "Fine, I will track and capture your fallen one, but after that, you forget about me. Do we have a deal?"

Uriel laughed and bowed. "We have a deal. I'll fly you to where she was last seen, and then pray to me when you've got her and I'll come." The archangel turned and walked away, knowing that Samson would just go on using his skill to murder people for money. *Maybe I'll let Michael know where he is and let him deal with his own mess,* he thought as he exited the building and spread his wings. He smiled as he waited for Samson to gather some things and knew it was almost done.

SAFE HAVEN

Eve sat on the mound of dirty blankets and couldn't help but feel relaxed. The place was stuffy, for a bolt hole, and stank to high heavens—no pun intended. Yet, for all of that, it was comfy and she couldn't deny that she needed this to recover from everything she had been through. It was little more than a bunch of thick cardboard boxes taped together in back of the stout bushes in the park. The outside was covered in branches to avoid simple detection, and the smell was masked by the thick clover that grew around the outside. Eve suspected that people knew of its existence, but ignored it on general principles on account of its occupant.

"Tea?" Jobe asked, offering her a flask.

She eyed the container with a raised eyebrow but took it anyway. *I could use something stronger anyway.* She took a pull and wasn't disappointed. The harsh taste of bourbon washed down her throat and it warmed her insides as it travelled. "That's some 'tea' Jobe."

"Water, wine, who cares as long as it warms you up, right?"

Eve stretched her arms and stood, amazed that she could stand in this small box. She could've sworn that it was cramped a minute ago. *Stuff is stronger than I thought.* She was about to head outside for some air when she heard the unmistakable sound of wings flapping above them. Not the minute wings of any avian native to this world, no. These were the massive wings of an angel she was hearing; and if she could hear them, then they were in trouble. She grabbed Jobe and pulled him down to the floor putting one finger to her lips to make sure he was quiet, yet he laughed and stood once more.

"Don't worry, Eve, they can't find us in here. I told you it was safe." Jobe proclaimed quite loudly.

Panic set in as she imagined what they would do to the poor homeless man that had shown her kindness. *If only I had a sword*, she thought, *or some other weapon.* Then, as if the old man was telling the truth, the sound of wings departed and silence reigned. "What? How?" It was then that she placed his accent. It seemed like Israeli, and early at that. Yet he was talking with some weird American slang

"How? Well, you could say that someone wants you kept safe and that, in the end, you will save someone very important to Him," the man called Jobe said, standing a little straighter. Besides, I was getting bored down here anyway; no one listens to me anymore, not like the old days." He motioned for her to sit and did so himself, bringing another flask out from behind his back. "I used to be such a hit with the people, sitting under a tree and talking about Him all day long."

Eve knew then who she was in the company of, yet it couldn't be. "You can't be *him*," she said, her voice reflecting her doubt. "He was *mortal* and ascended to heaven eons ago."

Jobe chuckled. "I am mortal, yes. Dying does wonders for the soul you know. Big guy could've at least warned me about that one," the man who wasn't Jobe smiled. "You see, after the calamity, He sent me back to guide humanity. It isn't their fault that they are so distrusting. No one believed who I was, so I became Jobe. It helped a bit. Yet, I still haven't hit the target audience like I used to." The man took off some of the decrepit rags and clothes and beneath was a simple white robe, unstained by any filth.

Eve chuckled at who had guided her here to recover from her ordeals. "Of all the people to save me, I never thought it would be *you*."

"Well, you know the old saying...Jesus saves." The man that was once the King of Man turned and sat on a filthy pile of bags and kicked his feet out, lighting a pipe. "Stay here for a couple days and recover, you'll be safe from all eyes for now, then you can rush out towards your destiny. Sound fair?"

"As long as you keep that tea coming," Eve said with a smile.

"Oh, I think I can handle that trick, though I do have to travel north in a couple days to find an old friend."

The Devil's in the Details

The man sat back in his chair and whistled slowly at the news. "You are sure of this description?" Natasha asked as his slick blond hair dangled in front of his hazel eyes. He smoothed out his Armani suit and stood, concern written on his angelic face.

"Yes sir, it was a man the size of a mountain with olive skin and very long, brown braids. He was wearing jeans and no shirt, covered in tattoos."

Natasha dismissed his underling and paced the small, run-down office. *I really need to relocate these guys,* he thought, looking out the broken window at the rubble of Old Chicago. *Upgrade the cult, so-to-speak.* Sadly, he didn't have time for that right now. If it was truly the man he knew, then Eve was in serious trouble. And he still couldn't locate her. *Well, if I can't then Samson can't either, I guess,* Natasha thought as he walked to the door.

"Shall I get the car, Natasha?" one of the men asked as he opened the door.

Natasha sighed, and then nodded with a smile. *Now I remember why I work alone*, he thought. *You never have a moment's peace with a cult.* He checked his watch and picked up his pace. It was time to get into this personally. *Besides, it's been too long since I talked to Samson, my third favorite mortal to corrupt, next to Delilah and Eve.* Natasha, or Lucifer as he was more infamously known, walked out and got in his car, driving off towards the horizon to meet his fate.

No Rest for the Wicked

WALKING

The oddly dressed man limped down the cobblestone path of the garden and couldn't help but reflect on the beauty of what these people had rebuilt, even though he hated most of them. His robes were ancient and outdated, seeming more akin to a medieval play than what one would wear on a warm spring afternoon in the Forests of Vermont. Various charms and adornments clattered against his side as he walked, swinging by their own gruesome hangings from chains around his waist. There were bags, a box, and even dozens of individual keys.

Two women walked by him and smiled. He tipped his wide brimmed hat at them and offered a return smile through his long beard. However, the smile never touched his cold, mismatched eyes—one blue and one green. The fallen angel Nergal had been walking this world for eons, ever since his fall from heaven, yet had been lost for many years after the calamity these humans did to themselves. His body had been destroyed that day, but a deal with the devil had gotten him a new one. The body of Marcus Brant was a little beat up, but with a wardrobe change and a new hat, Nergal was back in the swing of things again.

Nergal had lost his body when he fell from grace, just like Belial had, and he had been possessing other bodies to blend in, wearing faces to mask his true nature. This had earned him the nickname "Legion" way back in the day. Ever since he acquired this body, though, he didn't need to do that anymore. It felt so good to be whole once more. He stopped at the gate of the dark path he was looking for and glanced up at the massive trees on either side, once again impressed at what had been saved from the dark days.

Humanity had broken their world decades ago and had tried to rebuild here and there, but the New England City States had to be the best of them all. The individual states of New Hampshire, Vermont, Maine, and Massachusetts came together after the catastrophe and set aside all differences to create a safe haven for the people. They built a wall around their borders and rebuilt their cities towards the central part of the area, letting nature take back the edges. These massive forests, like the one he was currently in, were patrolled by packs of Hunters, the official guard of the N.E.C.S.

Nergal walked on past the gate and could hear the sounds of the deeper woods echoing around him. He usually avoided places with animals because they could sense him while others could not. But, he was repaying a favor for an old friend and didn't want to irritate her-not that he considered Lilith a friend-but still. She had found him in the ruins of Chicago and asked him to find the archangel Ariel and deliver a package. He owed her for saving him eons back when he had been cast into a pig's body; this would wipe that debt clean. Nergal hadn't looked inside the bag she gave him and, in truth, really didn't want to know what Lilith would be sending their long lost sister anyway. Besides, it kept moving. It had taken him months to track down where Ariel could be, and the trip had taken a little longer than normal-getting used to this new body and all after Belial had almost ruined it for him in the fight with Lucifer. Now he had finally arrived; wouldn't she be surprised to see him.

Back to Work

Ariel spun lazily around the tree and laughed at the large man trying to catch her. She ran her fingers through her long brown hair, strands the color of the very earth she walked upon, and spun once more, dodging his grasp. As she twirled, her green shawl spun out like a fan and she danced backwards. Yet, the big man's hand grabbed her faded jeans and pulled her towards his embrace. Ariel was the archangel of nature and had met the man awhile ago, the two of them hitting it off instantly.

"I have you now," the man said in his deep voice. He wore faded jeans of his own and sported a tight white t-shirt. His jacket looked worn and very old, like it was his grandfather's, and his piercing eyes were the color of wet dirt—a deep brown that seemed made of the very earth itself. He had long, brown hair and tanned skin, on a massive frame filled with corded muscle. Cain smiled as he held her tightly to him, and breathed in her earthy scent like he needed it to survive, maybe he did. Cain was the oldest being on the earth and had been cursed since the day he killed his own brother, Abel. He had been many things over the millennia, but he was trying to change. Over the last hundred years, he had saved a lot of people. Yet, had never truly felt happy-until he met Ariel.

"You only *think* you have me," Ariel replied with a smile of her own as she licked his face and released her deep brown wings at the same time. When he relaxed his grip, she burst free and took to the air, laughing. She would've normally been invisible with her wings out, but Cain was cursed-so he could still see her.

Cain bounded at a tree and leapt up, grabbing a low-hanging branch. Pulling himself up, he kicked off and soared after her, latching onto her foot and dragging her back down to earth with him. They landed in a heap, laughing uncontrollably as they tussled. Cain finally pinned her under his massive bulk and kissed her passionately as he held her hands clasped in one of his own above her head in the moss. As they broke, he smiled down into her eyes. "Have I ever thanked you?" he asked quietly, his sincerity catching her off guard.

"For what, Love?" Ariel asked as she lay there under him. She had fallen for him completely after their encounter with Lilith and she had brought him here to the Forests of Vermont to rest and relax from the world around them. The days had been pure bliss for her, especially since she had never truly been in love before.

"For finding me and bringing me here...with you."

"There is nothing to thank me for. It was selfish of me anyway."

"Why selfish?"

"Because I can't be happy without you by my side anymore," Ariel confessed with a coy smile of her own.

"You two make me sick," a voice called out from behind them.

Visitor

Cain rolled with Ariel and they both leapt to their feet. The first murderer stepped in front of her and leveled his cold eyes at the intruder. "Who are you, stranger, and what do you want?"

"I've had many names—this body having once been called Marcus Brant—but she would know me as Nergal," the fallen angel replied with a sneer. "Long time no see, sis."

Ariel sniffed and said nothing as she walked around to the side.

Cain laughed, keeping his stance but relaxing his shoulders. "Ah, I know that name as well, though I prefer you as a pig, or was it pigs, plural."

His mismatched eyes narrowing, Nergal took a step forward but stopped, his fists clenching at his side. "This is none of your concern, Cain."

"All right, Nergal, I'll bite. What do you want?" Ariel knew something important had to be up for him to be seeking her out. He hated them all for what happened to him...and she couldn't say she blamed him overmuch. It seemed truly horrible to be insubstantial.

"Call off your dog first, sis, and I'll talk."

Before Cain could act Ariel rushed in front of the big man and laid her hand on his chest. She closed her eyes and sent tendrils of warmth into him, soothing his rage. She felt him take a deep breath and relax, and then she turned towards her fallen brother and frowned, her deep brown eyes narrowing to match his own look. "First of all *he* is not my *dog*...Felix is." The archangel of nature pointed to the right without even glancing that way and a huge creature emerged from the brush. The wolf was three times the size of a normal wolf and the toothy grin that it sported gleamed in the sunlight coming down from above. "And before you think it," she went on without pause, "I have even more friends behind you. This is *my* safe place, Nergal, and I choose who gets in and gets out."

Cain just smiled and ran his hand over the wolf's neck as it came over to them. He had never been useless before, it felt good to not be needed for once.

"Settle down, Ariel, I know you are in charge here." Nergal took off a bag from his chain belt and dropped it on the mossy forest floor, then backed away slowly. "And before you ask-no, I don't know what it is."

"Who told you to bring it?" Cain asked as Ariel walked forward. He had a bad feeling about this and the timing of it all.

"Look, I did a favor for Lucifer and got this body from Belial. Then, after a few weeks, Lilith found me and called in *her* debt. I'm delivering this to cancel that debt to Lilith," Nergal said calmly, his smile gone now as he looked around him. "You know, don't shoot the messenger and all that."

Ariel knelt down and pulled the string on the package as it moved on its own slightly.

The hair on the back of Cain's neck stood straight up and he lunged forward, shoving Ariel out of the way of the bag as it flew open. A blur struck from the inside of the bag and Cain felt the sting on his arm as Ariel hit the ground and rolled. Cain smiled over at her as the snake pumped him full of its lethal toxin. He recognized the small scales and yellow coloring of the Western Taipan, or inland Taipan. His lungs were already seizing and his muscles locked up as he fell to his knees. He wouldn't die—he was cursed to live forever—but he could feel every death he had and they all took their toll on him.

"Cain...Cain stay with me!" Ariel called out, but her voice was fading quickly.

"It's all...right..." Cain tired to say but everything was so far away.

Trapped

Ariel looked up as Cain stopped breathing, tears falling down her face. She had felt the last beat of his heart and it snapped something deep inside of her. Nergal was already backing away, looking nervously from side to side as she stood very slowly, all compassion gone from her beautiful face.

"I didn't know that was in there," Nergal said desperately as she advanced upon him. "You have to believe me."

"You have finally gone too far, Nergal," Ariel said as she pointed to him and nodded. "Messenger or not, you have crossed my line and your own luck has run out." A huge figure, easily eight feet tall, stepped out from behind the fallen angel and lunged for Nergal-its massive hands clutching for him. The thing was covered in fur and had an intelligence to its fierce eyes.

Nergal leapt aside, waving his hand at the creature. The thing tripped into a tree, momentarily stunning it.

"Your powers of bad luck will only serve to make him angry, dear brother," Ariel said without emotion. Her heart was cold right now, beating in a chest that had a void in it. This was all new to her and she was being overwhelmed with it all. Her heart cried out for vengeance and her fallen brother was the outlet. "Besides, I know you will just find another body-and I've heard someone is looking for you, so you had better hide when you do."

"Listen, Ariel, we can just..." Nergal would've said more, but the creature grabbed his neck in its massive hands and squeezed with all its strength, cutting off the rest of what the fallen angel was trying to say. The creature twisted those hands quickly and, with a loud snap, the body of Nergal went limp. A faint scream could be heard on the wind as Nergal's spirit flew off in the distance. Marcus Brant's body could finally rest in peace. The creature bowed and lumbered off into the deep woods once more, fading back into myth and legend.

Ariel bent down and ran her hand over the snake as it started to curl around her foot. It never would've bitten her and Lilith knew that. No. That demon bitch knew Cain would protect her and wanted him out of the way for some other reason...but why? She searched the bag for some other clue as to why Lilith would send her this when she saw the note. It was addressed to her and sealed with black wax. *She was always so dramatic, that one,* Ariel thought as she opened it.

Dearest sister:

I know that you have no cause to trust me right now, but Cain is needed in New Dallas again. Uriel has hired Samson, of all people, and the only one that can stop that murderer is Cain. I know you will think this is some scheme, but I hate Samson more than I loathe you. Besides, I'm trying to get on Lucifer's good side and this might help

Lilith

Ariel crumpled the note and wiped her tears. She knew that Cain would survive but it still tore her heart that he had to suffer for anyone. *How can these mortals do this?* she thought as she felt the pain in her heart for the man on the ground. *Every day they lose the ones they love and have to feel this?* Father could be cruel in some ways and she had always hated that side of Him. *Still, everything happens for a reason,* she thought as she looked upon the man she had grown to love over the past couple of months. It hit her then why the snake was sent; Cain would've never believed the note. Sighing loudly at what she knew she must do, Ariel left her own note, scrawled into the bark of a dead tree so that Cain could find it when he arose. Once she was done, she unfurled her wings and flew off, crying fresh tears as she soared into the sky. She didn't know if she would ever see him again.

ΠEW Paths

Cain came around with a deep intake of air and rolled to his feet. Everything hurt and there was a thin covering of moss growing on his clothes. *How long was I out for that time?* he asked himself as he looked around the clearing. He noticed the wolf lying by a huge dead tree and frowned. He saw no sign of Ariel. "Where is she, boy?" he asked playfully, smiling at the thought of her. When the wolf laid its head down and whimpered Cain's gut twisted in knots. That was when he saw the note on the tree.

Cain,

I've gone to New Dallas to help my brother, catch up with me when you can

Love, Ariel

He grinned and turned, setting out quickly. It would take him a bit to get to civilization, but he would find her and help, then come back here and finally put everything behind him and be happy. *Or finally die trying*

Nergal walked briskly across the grass and looked behind him for the hundredth time. The body he had found was wearing out quickly and he had no faces to blend in. Curse Ariel for taking away the body he just got, and curse Lilith for sending him to his doom. This is exactly why he hated everyone! The archangel of nature had told him someone was after him, and he couldn't imagine who it could be, but over the last couple of days he had seen someone just out of the corner of his eye following him. Try as he might, he just couldn't catch a good look, only a flitting imagine of a man. He had thrown bad luck the man's way, but nothing happened, which was bad.

Normally Nergal wouldn't even worry about such things, nothing on this earth could kill him permanently, yet if an archangel knew someone was looking for him...then they weren't of this earth. He was so preoccupied with looking behind him that he turned down a street and ran into a wall shortly afterwards. *Damn it all to hell,* he thought, rubbing the bruise on his head. *I turned down a side street.* The irony of his prey always turning down these very streets was not lost on him. Before he could even turn and walk back out a man cleared his throat behind him.

"Long time no see, Nergal," the man said in perfect Aramaic.

Nergal froze at the sound of the voice and the language used. "It *can't* be you," he whispered as he finally did turn to see the man stalking him.

"I've been looking for you."

"Jesus Christ," the fallen angel swore as he turned and attempted to scale the wall he ran into. The crumbling bricks and dirt hindering his progress.

"No. I go by Jobe these days," the man said now in perfect English. He wore white robes with no shoes and his brown hair blended perfectly with his olive skin. Brown eyes shone with mischief as the man slowly brought a small cage out from behind his back, low growls of some animal within echoing in the shrouded alley.

Nergal wasted no time with banter. He had to flee before the man cast him out and into whatever was in that cage. *Not again...I won't survive the mind of a lesser being again...I can't!* The sound of Jobe's voice chanting the phrases of the verse that would exorcise him drove him on to almost pure panic. His fingers bled as he scraped his way up and almost over the wall, he gripped the edge of the wall and pulled with everything he had as he felt the tug of his very spirit. "No...please!" then he froze... his lifeless body dropping over to the other side and landing in a heap.

Inside the cage, the mangy cat wailed and scratched the inside of the little plastic jail to no avail. Nergal, now in the body of the cat, could hear Jobe whistling as they walked on down the street and he could only wonder what he was in for. He could feel his mind shrinking to fit the tiny mind of the animal he now inhabited and he retreated inside that mind with the only words that got him through the last time...*I am not alone, I am Legion.*

Jobe walked into the pet store and rang the little bell on the counter, the cage in his hand swinging wildly with the angry occupant.

"How can I help you today, stranger?" The friendly owner asked in a squeaky voice. She had on a cross necklace and thick glasses.

"I have this cat that I can no longer care for. Is there any way I could give her to you?"

"We don't buy pets, mister. I'm sorry."

"Oh, I don't want money, just a good home for the little fellow."

"Really? Well, in that case maybe I can find a place for the little guy." She bent down and peered into the cage, pulling back when the cat hissed and attacked the locked door. "Feisty, isn't he?"

"He can be a real demon sometimes," Jobe answered truthfully. He took out a small collar and placed it on the counter

"Is that a tiny cross on that collar?"

"Good eye. Yes, it is." Jobe put the cage on the counter and opened the door slowly, grabbing the cat by the neck firmly before it could escape. "It's actually made from Jerusalem wood and has been in my family for a very long time." He took the collar and put it on the cat, then set the mangy cat down.

"Well, would you look at that. Calm as a cucumber." The woman petted the cat slowly and smiled as it started to purr.

"He should be fine as long as that thing stays on...he gets really ornery without it."

"Why, thank you, stranger. Say, you seem awfully familiar. Don't you go to church down the street?"

Jobe smiled even wider and shook his head. "No, I'm not a fan of churches actually. I'm more of a sit in a field around people type of guy." He petted the cat one more time and took his leave, happy that he could put at least this one thing to rest for awhile.

Flight of the Fallen

FROM THE DARKNESS

He bent over the filthy puddle in the middle of the street and smiled; she had come this way and that meant he still had her trail. The man was huge, well over six feet tall and had long hair, which was braided down his back. The thick, brown locks complemented his olive skin and brown eyes. Samson was not known by any of these mortals anymore, yet if they had read their Bible, they would know who he was from his stories. Oh, sure, in Sunday school he was always the hero and famed for his great strength and tragic ending...but they always skipped over the many murders he had committed back then; the church was good for that. Samson stepped out into the night lights of New Dallas and smiled at the people bustling by him; they had no idea that greatness stood among them.

"Hey, buddy, you're going to get hit if you stay in the road like that." The voice belonged to a man in a worn suit, holding a brief case.

Samson took two large steps towards the man, grabbed him by his collar, and heaved him into the oncoming cars with ease. The squeal of brakes and shattered glass echoed across the night as the beat-up trucks and cars piled up. Parts—both mechanical and body—flew through the air as people screamed, drawing a small crowd. The big man casually walked on into the forming crowd after his quarry; he had no time for insolence this night.

Samson had been on the trail of this fallen angel for three weeks now and she had evaded him with a skill that he hadn't expected, almost like she had help from other people. *Like angels,* he thought, annoyed at the information that had been withheld from him by the one that contracted him. Uriel had told him to bring the girl to him, but it would've been easier if he had known what he was up against. He knew that her name was Evenal, currently going by Eve, and what she looked like, yet every time he had come close to catch her, she had slipped through his grasp.

As he came up upon the building where her trail led, he noticed that there was a light on three floors up. *Good. I can go up in darkness and have the element of surprise,* he thought as he snuck quietly into the building. Samson may well be a giant among men, but he was exceptionally stealthy for one of his size. He wasn't worried about resistance because the archangel Uriel had already told him that no living being would be able to thwart him in his pursuit; angels weren't technically alive, though, so he was in for a challenge. Two floors up he felt a tingle down his spine and turned, barely blocking a kick that sent him sliding backwards two feet.

"Oh, you are good," a deep voice remarked as the dark figure came at him again.

"I've had years of training," Samson quipped at the warrior as he advanced. This was no novice assassin he faced. The man was well trained and very powerful, which surprised him, mainly because of Uriel's prediction.

"I'm well aware of your extensive murders; I've got quite the body count as well, old man." The dark assassin stepped closer and smiled, showing long white fangs that protruded from his mouth.

Well, Uriel wasn't wrong...this thing isn't alive either, Samson thought. "It's been a while since I've killed a vampire," he said, going into a stance that favored quick strikes and throws. He knew that Eve would get away now, but that was fine...he would find her again after he dealt with this annoyance.

"I've heard that before," the vampire said, ducking around Samson with preternatural speed. "And I'm still here."

"I'm shocked to see one of your kind in New Dallas. They don't take kindly to vampires. What's in this for you?" Samson asked, measuring the creature's steps and speed. If he could keep him talking, he could land one decisive blow and end it quickly.

"I owe a debt to Lucifer and this will set me free from that." The vampire smiled once more then surged forward lashing out with his claws and a kick.

Samson blocked the claws but took the kick hard, hearing two ribs crack under the force of the creature's blow. One...two...step...now. Samson spun with his arm down low and came up with everything he had, catching the creature in the neck. The vampire sailed through the air and hit the cement wall with such force that blood poured out of his mouth, the stolen vitae spilling onto the dusty ground. The fractured body quivered as the thing tried to stand, but Samson was right there in a heartbeat, lifting it up by a leg and an arm. With a great heave of his massive chest, he ripped the vampire in two, drenching himself in blood and ending the vile creature's existence. Contrary to rumors and stories, vampires could be killed without stakes and silver. Cutting off the head, or even dismembering them like this, was enough to sever their cursed spirits forever-leaving them wandering ghosts like the rest of the lost souls of this earthly Hell. Samson stood there basking in the kill and his thoughts drifted to his quarry and who was helping her. *Lucifer has a hand in this as well? This could be more fun than I thought.*

On the Run

She ran down the street as night fell on the city, on the run since she had fallen from Heaven. And although she hated hiding and running like this, she wouldn't have changed anything she had done. She was supposed to kill two innocent boys that had found love and, in that moment, when she had disobeyed the order from an archangel, she had been sent down in flames, her wings burning away and scales covering her arms. She used to go by Evenal, but now she just went by Eve.

Eve risked a look back at the abandoned building she had been hiding in and saw the light still on. *I wonder if it worked,* she thought as she jogged down the street in darkness. She was just about to eat when the dark assassin had come to her and told her to run. Eve hadn't seen a vampire in centuries, so it had taken her by surprise. However, if the man that was after her was who she thought it was, she might well be in trouble this time.

A vampire wouldn't slow down Samson at all, not with the strength that his long hair bestowed him, that-and immortality. She had been told by the archangel Gabriel that someone was looking out for her and would find her soon, but that was three weeks ago and she was getting tired of running. She couldn't take Samson though, not with his skill and strength, so running was her only option. Eve turned down an alley without thinking, lost in her thoughts, and realized too soon that it was a dead end.

"What do we 'ave here, lads?" a drunken voice called out from behind her as she turned. The man was standing in the entranceway with three other men, all dressed in cheap suits and holding makeshift weapons. They seemed like typical New Dallas thugs protecting their turf. The city might well be a modern heaven to its citizens, but the dark side of humanity thrived here as well. "I think we've stumbled upon some fun this evening."

Eve wouldn't have normally worried about the odds like this before, but she was tired and run down; this could be bad. "You really don't want to do this, guys," she started to say, yet something drew their attention away from her. The men all turned as another figure came around the corner into the alley from behind them.

"Now now, gentlemen, I am sure you only wanted to escort the young lady to a safer place," the man said, his voice like silk in the growing darkness. As he came, forward his dark, finely tailored suit was a stark contrast to the suits the men were wearing. He had blond hair and green eyes that seemed to bore into your very soul, as well they should, considering who he was.

Eve recognized him as the man that saved her months ago when she had been caught by Belial. It was Lucifer himself! The men turned on him and laughed, hefted their weapons, and advanced upon him without banter or pause. Lucifer looked over them to her and winked, mouthing the word 'run' as he dropped into a stance and moved among them like Death itself. He was no Michael; yet, this was the devil himself and these humans had absolutely zero chance of surviving this encounter. She turned and ran around them as he went after them with a speed that astounded her. He was fluid and graceful, striking without mercy, and landing blows that took out his opponents with ease. By the time she was back into the street, they were all down and incapacitated.

"Well, that was a good workout," Lucifer said coming up beside her. He was fixing his cufflinks and smiling. Thankfully he had finally replaced the one he gave to young Simon, as it brought his whole ensemble together—at least in his mind.

"Luci..." she started, yet he stopped her with a raised finger.

"Natasha."

"Sorry. Natasha, why did you save me again?"

"Well, let's just say that I have an interest in your continued freedom and leave it at that."

"Fair enough." Eve wanted to press him for more details—the look he was giving her made her blush for some reason—but they had to move before that massive human caught her trail once more. "So, where to?"

"Oh, I have a cute little bar I'm taking you to. You'll absolutely love it," The archangel currently going by Natasha said as he snaked his arm through hers and picked up the pace.

"What about the thing chasing me?"

"Oh, you mean Samson? I left a note as to where we will be so he can go there."

"Won't he know it's a trap?" Eve knew that no mortal being was a match for an archangel, but still this was Samson.

"Oh, he will definitely know it's a trap. You see I'm sending him to the bar called Delilah."

"You're evil," Eve said laughing at the name. "But won't we stick out a bit in a place like that?"

"Oh, we're not going there, I'm just sending him there as a little message to leave me alone." Natasha laughed again and walked on, arm in arm with Eve, down the street. "He hates to be stood up but I'm not in the mood to deal with him at the moment."

"This is going to be fun, isn't it?" Eve asked as she stared at the man next to her. He was handsome and charming, all the things she never thought the devil would be. He only winked in reply.

Coming Together

Natasha was bothered. He entered the Black Claw bar with his usual swagger, the fallen angel Eve on his arm, yet his mind was wildly distracted. He had been watching out for this little fallen one for awhile now and he found something different about her every time he laid his eyes upon her. She was a fighter, a hardened warrior that defied Father and had paid the price. She was also lithe and quick, as well as fierce and kind and...*Get it together*, he admonished himself as they approached the bar. Natasha was dressed in his usual black Armani suit complete with silver cufflinks, and his blond hair hung just over his deep hazel eyes. "Two whiskeys straight," he said to the rough looking female bartender staring at them.

"I think you have the wrong place, mister," she said looking them over and pointing to the rest of the clientele. The bar was dark and full of bikers wearing leather and chains. In these new days of the fallen world, gangs had flourished as roaming warriors out on the desolate roads and they always looked for fights when they were bored.

Here in New Dallas, they came together to take on contracts, often protecting caravans of supplies.

"Oh, I'm not worried, good lady, just pour the drinks and take your payment," Natasha said, his gaze turned fully on her now. The barkeep couldn't meet that gaze. Not many could, when he put his mind to it, and she went to pour the drinks.

"What are we doing here, Natasha," Eve asked as she also looked around the room.

"There is someone we are meeting here who will deal with Samson for us so we can be rid of his annoying presence." Natasha took his whiskey and downed it, sliding the bartender a gold coin. The woman took it and almost dropped it, then hurried to the back to hide it away. It was worth almost as much as the building they stood in.

"Who is this mysterious acquaintance?" Eve asked, as she, too, shot back her drink and slammed the glass down.

"That would be me," a voice answered from behind them.

Eve turned and had to look up. The man staring down at her was dressed in faded jeans and a tight white t-shirt. His jacket looked worn and very old, like it was his grandfathers, and his piercing eyes were the color of wet dirt, a deep brown that seemed made of the very earth itself. He had long brown hair and tanned skin on a massive frame filled with corded muscle. "Oh, shit."

"Oh shit, indeed," Cain said as he took a seat next to them at the bar.

"Good to see you, Adam," Natasha said hailing the barkeep once more. All eyes were on them now, and more than one person had stood with some sort of weapon in their hands; the gang didn't like people on their turf.

"I'm going by Cain for now, until I can find Ariel and put Lilith in the ground for good."

"Well, that sounds like a fun show. Do let me know and I'll bring the popcorn," Natasha said as the barkeep poured more drinks. He slammed back his and slid one towards Cain.

"Um...guys?" Eve said as she finished her own drink again. "We may have company soon."

"We should go in the back soon," Cain said. "That is unless you want me to kill everyone in here?"

"I've got another idea," Natasha said as he took out another coin and walked forward with a grace than betrayed his power. "Now now, gentleman, this pure gold coin goes to whoever is left standing." He spun it up into the air and stepped back as it came down on a table, the sound echoing in the sudden silence. The coin hit the table and spun, almost by magic. All at once the crowd surged forward and blows landed among them as each one fought to grasp the coin of the devil. It would literally change someone's life, for ill or good, and Natasha led his friends to the back of the bar as the patrons clawed each other apart to get it.

"You never change, Satan," Cain said laughing as they entered a private room.

"I hate that name," Natasha said, making a face as he said it. "Damn Catholics and their name calling; bunch of bullies is what they are."

"Can we pretend to be adults for a second and figure this out?" Eve asked as she sat down and crossed her scaled arms. The black scales were a side effect of falling from heaven and covered the upper arms and legs.

"There is nothing to figure out. Cain is here to take care of Samson and we are going to go find Gabriel and settle this with Uriel."

"And find Ariel," Cain interjected.

"I'll see if I can get a hold of her, Cain," Natasha said with a smile. He knew that Ariel had led him here and that it was breaking her heart not to be with him, but they needed Cain to stop Samson.

Cain simply nodded.

"No offense, Cain, but can you take Samson?" Eve asked. She knew that Cain was the oldest human on the planet, and the first murderer, yet Samson was the epitome of strength.

"I think I can handle my offspring," Cain said with a smile that never touched his cold eyes. "He is good, but I've been doing this awhile myself."

"He is your offspring?"

Natasha laughed and patted Eve on the shoulder. "Yes, most of the major figures of the ancient days have this man's blood running through them, dear. Not directly, but back then bloodlines blended rather easily." He looked down at her again and felt a pang of regret. Once this was finished, she would go off on her own and he would never be able to admire her again. *Why does that bother me?* he asked himself as he walked over to peak out into the main room. Only three individuals were left, including the bartender. The greedy woman was reloading a shotgun as another pulled a hidden knife. Some people just couldn't walk away when they were ahead.

"All right, so you two get going and I'll head to Delilah's and catch up with Samson." Cain bowed to Eve and shook the devil's hand, then walked out among the chaos.

Anticipation

Eve walked out of the ruined bar with Lucifer, or Natasha as he liked to be called now, and marveled at the empty streets. That much fighting and death should've brought the enforcers, yet there was no one in sight.

"Where are the Rangers?" Eve asked as she looked around.

"Oh, well, I knew that we would probably cause a scene so I paid them off. They'll show up in about an hour or so to clean up," Natasha said, taking her arm again. "Ready?" Natasha asked as he turned to her and unfurled his glorious white wings. The only fallen angel to retain them in existence, it was rumored that he had kept them because he was thrown down, not actually fallen by choice- like she had.

The anticipation of finally being free was a palpable thing on her scaled skin. Eve stepped into his embrace without pause and they soared upward into the sky. *I didn't even hesitate to be held by the Devil,* she thought as she tried to figure out why she felt completely safe. He had been watching over her for so long that she just assumed that he wouldn't ever hurt her and that feeling was extremely new to her. She even found herself burying her head in his neck as they flew out over the land, the ruined houses and buildings quickly passing them by underneath.

In no time, they were setting down in a field somewhere in the Field State of Oklahoma, white flowers growing as far as the eye could see. The Field State of Oklahoma was an abandoned place of empty farms and wild fields that served as a reminder of how the world used to be. Other than the occasional town or village, nothing was left here except rusty farming equipment and miles of overgrown fields that served as breeding grounds for wild flowers. These pastures were rumored to have been blessed by God Himself; Standing in them right now, Eve couldn't say they were wrong. She had seen His Grace, been a part of it for eons, and this was close. Then she saw who was waiting for them.

The archangel Gabriel was leaning on a rusty tractor, his white suit looking like it came right off the rack. He had long dirty blond hair and green eyes like liquid emeralds that sparkled in the sunlight. "Well, I see you two finally met up," Gabriel said as he walked forward, taking Eve's hand and kissing it.

Eve blushed slightly and noticed that Natasha seemed irritated by the gesture. Smiling at the thought of the devil being jealous, she bowed to Gabriel and had to admit that standing together, they seemed a mirror image. Both had the same hair and eyes, yet one dressed in white while the other preferred black. "So, what happens now?"

Natasha smiled. "Now we go find Uriel and end this."

His Greatest Fear

Date with Destiny

He felt his shoes sink into the soft mud and scowled as he walked through the drenched field. It had been raining for over an hour now and his brown hair fell into his eyes as the water dripped down his face. This was just another instance that he loathed being down here among the humans rather than in Heaven where he belonged. The archangel Uriel stopped and looked up into the dark clouds soaring overhead and frowned more deeply. He knew that they would be waiting for him and that they thought they had him figured out...little did they know that he was one step ahead of his brothers. Oh, sure, they were powerful, too—one never took Lucifer for granted—but to see his brother Gabriel working with the fallen angel truly turned his heart cold. All for the stupid fate of a fallen angel named Evenal.

Evenal, or Eve as she was going by this last year, had refused to eliminate two young lovers and, in so doing, broke her vow and fell from grace. Her wings lost, she was on the run from Uriel's hunters who were bound to bring her back to heaven for reconditioning. Once Uriel had her back home, he could go back to doing what he loved...watching the patterns of these frail mortals and taking the loose threads out so they flourished. Uriel looked around as he neared the dilapidated farm house where Lucifer, Gabriel, and Evenal, had met and smiled-the effect never touching his eyes in the slightest. They had left traces of their presence for him to follow, as if he wouldn't know anyway. *They're mocking me at this point*, he thought as he walked on through the ruined field. There were flowers everywhere, taking over land after the humans had wrecked everything with their impudence. They had broken their world years ago and now nature was taking things back. He stopped as a distant noise drew his attention, a faint thud felt through the very earth as if some weight had impacted nearby. He unfurled his silver wings and walked on, curious as to what this could be.

As Uriel walked around the ruined, farmhouse he caught sight of the disturbance and frowned even more deeply. Two massive figures fought it out among the pouring rain, neither giving nor taking quarter. They both looked tattered and bruised, covered in blood and filth, yet neither showed signs of fatigue. One of the men had a long brown braid hanging down his bruised back, his massive fists landing blow after blow upon the forearm of the other. The mighty warrior Samson was skilled beyond the years of mortal men and had stopped aging a thousand years before the coming of Christ. His hair gave him strength, yet even that could not prevail over his opponent. The other man was just as big, his frame sporting muscles that had been honed since the very first days of the earth. There was no better fighter on the planet and the man had been killing since then. Cain, the first murderer, took the blows on his arm and returned them twofold, slamming Samson into the earth with such force that parts of the nearby house were coming down.

Cain shouldn't be able to defeat Samson, Uriel thought as his mind raced at the implications. *I saw that no living being would be able to thwart him in his pursuit.* Uriel watched the ill-fated match with curiosity now, wondering if Cain counted as a living being since he was immortal as well. *One more thing I missed,* he chided himself. It looked like they had been going at it for hours and over a long distance. as there seemed to be a trail of destruction through the field behind them. *They probably fought all the way from New Dallas.* Uriel had hired Samson to capture Eve; once again, they had found a way to thwart him. *No matter, I still have the upper hand.* Uriel walked on ignoring the two warriors and followed the trail left by his brothers. He knew what would happen, just not exactly when or why. That was his little gift-glimpses of the future. He had seen Eve fall and being brought to heaven in these patterns, so it was only a matter of time before he won.

Ariel flew down in the rain, her wings soaked and barely keeping her aloft. Lucifer had prayed to her and let her know that Cain had taken Samson off Eve's trail and that it was good to go to him once more. Now, she just hoped he had survived the battle. She heard them before she saw them, the titanic fight raging for hours across the heartland. Ariel landed in the mud and piles of destroyed flowers and pulled her wings in, shaking her hair out. She looked through the sheet of rain and saw the two men trading blows in the filth.

Samson looked hurt and weary—finally—but Cain looked worse. He was favoring an arm and limping, obviously hurt but not backing down. Ariel could feel his rage from here, probably the only thing keeping him upright at this point, given his injuries.

"Give up, old man!" Samson cried as he grabbed Cain's head and kicked his injured leg. "You can't match my strength."

Cain howled as his leg snapped, dropping him into the mud. His good arm shot out and grabbed Samson's foot as the man kicked again and he tossed it high, sending the man sprawling down with him. With the rage flooding him there were no words, no witty banter, nor cutting jabs-just violence. Cain lunged and grabbed Samson's shoulders, pinned the man down into the mud, and brought his own head down hard, head butting the warrior once, twice, then a third time.

Samson threw Cain off with a growl, but he was slow to stand now. His legendary endurance and strength were finally reaching their limit. He got to his feet, just in time to catch a broken piece of plow in the gut as Cain threw it.

"Enough of that, you two!" Ariel called out over the pouring rain. "End it or I will."

Samson turned and smiled, blood running out of his mouth making the gesture grim. "End this, slut," he called as he sent the plow at her face with everything he had left.

Ariel put up her arms and tried to dodge, but the heavy metal clipped her head and sent her sprawling.

"No!" Cain called through his rage. He stood on his broken leg and threw himself on Samson, rolling over and over as he punched and hit the warrior. "You won't hurt her!" He grabbed Samson by the hair and yanked back

hard, slamming his head down on the sharp metal of the broken plow. The long braid sheared off and before Samson could even say anything, Cain snapped his neck.

"Adam," Ariel said softly, her face already healed. "It's over now."

"I killed again," Cain said, ignoring the fact that she called him Adam.

"But you did it to save people this time."

"Is that justification enough?"

"It is for me," Ariel said wrapping her arms around him and holding him in the rain and mud. "Now, Adam, can we heal you up and go home?"

"Nothing would make me happier, Love."

Strange Feelings

He walked down the broken street and marveled at how nature had taken back this deserted town. The wind was blowing his blond hair into his hazel eyes and for once he didn't seem to mind. He was dressed in his Armani suit, complete with silver cuff links, and fit in with his surroundings like a prostitute at a nunnery. Natasha was in a good mood, though, and had high hopes that they would finally be free of all this hunting of fallen angels.

"You seem lost in thought today, brother," the man next to him said casually. "I've not known you to be so distracted." He, too, had dirty blond hair with emerald eyes; yet his attire was a white suit with polished shoes. They seemed two sides of a coin and indeed if anyone knew their real identity it would fit perfectly. The archangel Gabriel smiled at Natasha's scowl and laughed when their third companion barked laughter as well.

"That's rich, the devil lost in thought...what on the earth could keep his lustful attention for more than three seconds," the woman in-between them quipped as she pulled the long-sleeve shirt down over her scaly arms. Eve's skin had hardened into some sort of scales, almost like a dragon, and had turned a deep black to match her raven hair. Not as tall as the two archangels on either side of her, Eve was still a force to be reckoned with among mortals. Alas, that didn't do much when angelic hunters and an immortal biblical warrior were after her.

Natasha, who was actually the fallen archangel Lucifer, turned his gaze at her and his visage softened. *Why does her smile do that to me?* he asked himself for the hundredth time since first seeing her in Belial's back room. Ever since he had rescued her, he had been fascinated by her, even having people follow her and keep tabs on her. It was so unlike him that he had found himself making excuses...and he knew all about what that meant; he was the devil after all. "I'm just contemplating Uriel's next move, as well you both should," Natasha said with a flippant tone. "He won't fall for anything we try so the straightforward approach is all we have left."

Gabriel's expression hardened as he turned, stopping in the middle of an intersection. "He won't dare come against us both, brother, and with Samson busy, more than likely he will try and reason with us." Gabriel had to keep walking as Lucifer never stopped.

"Does that truly sound like Uriel?" Natasha kept walking, glad to have the upper hand with these two once again. He couldn't let them in on his weakness. He had to figure out why he was so drawn to this woman, she wasn't the most beautiful thing he had ever seen, or slept with for that matter, yet there was something about her that seemed...primal. *I just need to finish this and put some distance between us*, he thought, once again lying to himself. The devil just didn't have feelings for others...it just wasn't possible.

"No, it doesn't, though I haven't known him as intimately as you two have," Eve said as they neared their destination. "Why here, if I may ask?"

Natasha looked up at the cathedral they stood in front of and smiled. "This was one of the most treasured places of worship in the old days. It's only fitting that we meet here."

Gabriel snorted and walked on towards the ruined double doors, hanging by rusted screws and hinges long tarnished. "Well, we both know that these places did little to appease Father; they were for men-not God."

Natasha laughed and followed his brother into the broken-down place of worship. "Yes, but how easily they fell for it when I told them he would love it."

"Yeah, you were an ass back then," Gabriel said with a laugh.

Natasha couldn't refute that as he watched Eve walk into the cathedral. His eyes followed her every move and he tore his gaze away with effort. What was coming over him?

Fate's End

Uriel walked down the street towards the one place he knew they would be. Their trail went cold just after entering the ruined city. Regardless, he knew where they would be going. It was a mockery to meet him there, and no doubt they thought they were more than a match for him. They weren't wrong, yet he had something they didn't-knowledge. He had seen Eve impaled by a spear in some of the patterns, which was why he had recruited Samson, yet clearly that player had been taken out of the equation. Still, he had faith.

Uriel stopped at the steps and chuckled. They had no idea what he could do down here. His power had always been foresight-flashes of the future and what could be. Not as powerful as Lucifer's by any means, but knowledge was power, nonetheless. Since he came to earth, however, he could see more patterns and knew how to influence them. Knowing how things fit into a pattern was deadly when you knew what to move to cause things to spiral in the direction you want...and he knew just what to do.

"Don't stand out there all day, brother, come on in," Lucifer's voice echoed out of the open doors.

Uriel walked up the steps and into the house of the holy and moved three paces to the right, just under the statue of Mary. He saw a gigantic statue of Christ in the back, complete with the spear in his side, and smiled wider. Things were becoming clearer now. "Well, here we all are. Are you ready to go home, Evenal?" Predictably, Gabriel moved in front of her, pushing her behind his form as he smiled. Now she was just inches from where he needed her. One more thing and he had won.

"You don't stand a chance against both of us, Uriel," Gabriel said as he moved forward slowly.

"Oh, I have no intention of fighting either of you." Uriel drew a small dagger and tossed it lazily at Eve. She backed up as it clattered to the floor and Lucifer laughed.

"Your aim, brother, is as bad as your taste in clothes." The devil moved forward as well, slowly and at a pace with Gabriel.

Uriel drew another dagger and smiled, shrugging his shoulders. "I have no need to harm that fallen one, Lucifer, this unstable structure will do what I can't and then she will be home where she belongs." He looked up and threw the dagger with a strong arm this time, the blade turning end over end above all their heads. It hit the gigantic statue of Jesus and the crumbling structure groaned, breaking apart and coming down towards Eve.

"No!" Lucifer turned, his wings coming out in a blur as he flew towards her.

Uriel saw the statue come apart as the devil pushed her out of the way, catching the massive marble block on his back as it pinned him to the splintering floor. Eve fell on her back, her eyes wide as the marble spear that had been a part of the statue broke off and came crashing down into her stomach.

"What have you done, Uriel?" Gabriel screamed as he rushed to her side, his eyes closed and lips moving soundlessly.

"Praying for her, brother?" Uriel asked, walking forward now. He stopped when the statue pinning Lucifer down moved and fell to the side, the devil standing and looking at him with murderous intent. He could be in real trouble now.

"You, monster, will *pay* for that," Lucifer said, his eyes glowing an intense red.

"Natasha, she needs Raphael-now." Gabriel's voice was strained, no doubt from praying uselessly.

"Our sister won't be able to help her. Eve isn't human anymore than she is an angel. Only one place can heal that wound..." Uriel left the proclamation hanging in the stale air of the ruined chapel like the finality of the crumbling statue.

Lucifer picked up the frail, bloody body of eve, still somehow conscious, and scowled at the archangel. "She healed me just fine."

"Ah, Lucifer, you are a special case...see, you didn't fall." Uriel could see the devil's face drop as realization set in. "I see you understand now. Let me take her home and she will be fine." He held out his arms to receive his prize, but was shocked again when Lucifer flew straight up. "What is that fool *doing*?" Uriel couldn't believe his eyes. "He can't enter heaven; he'll burn this time for real!"

Gabriel fell to his knees as his brother flew through a hole in the ceiling and on toward Heaven. Silver tears fell silently as he looked up and smiled through those pure tears. "He knows that. Natasha has been struggling recently with his feelings for her and he just did the one thing no one thought he could ever do-not even him."

"What? What did he do?" Uriel was confused. Nothing in the patterns he had seen spoke of this.

"He is sacrificing himself for her...basically; he is admitting that he loves her." Gabriel stood and brushed his suit free of dust and spread his own wings. "Funny thing is, I'm not even sure he knows that himself."

"Wait, but I..."

"Uriel, I swear by Father's holy light, if you follow me, I will throw you down myself. You've caused enough problems; stay here for a while until this plays out. Then we can see how angry I will be with you later." Without another word to his brother, Gabriel flew up after Lucifer.

His Greatest Fear

Lucifer flew up through the clouds and held Eve tight against his chest. He could feel the tingling in his wings already, but he had made up his mind. If Uriel took her, she would be reconditioned and put back into the ranks like nothing ever happened, losing her sense of self. If he could get Michael's attention, though, maybe he could ask for his brother's help—if he didn't burn up first. The only thing that mattered was saving Eve.

"Nat...asha?" Eve's voice was barely a whisper, yet it got his attention. "Where are we? What are you doing?"

"Hush, now, I'm just bringing you home so they can fix you up."

"But..."

"You talk too much. Just hold on, all right?" Natasha said as he felt a tear fall down his beautiful face. He closed his eyes as he neared heaven and sparks started to flicker across his wings. Pain itched its way up his legs and his hands were turning black. Burn me all you want, *I won't let her die, Father....* His thoughts were prayers to the parent that had condemned him and for the first time in eons, a voice answered.

"You would die for her, son?"

The words hit him harder than any sword or hammer ever could. Would he? Natasha looked down at the girl in his arms, blood seeping more slowly now that she was almost gone, and a smile crept across his tear-streaked face. He had always feared opening up to anyone after the way Father had turned him away without a second thought...or how his brothers had thrown him out of his only home. Now, though, he realized that he would indeed die for her. "You can see into my cold, black heart, Father. You know I would." A bright light flared and Natasha winced, thinking it was the end. When the wind kept going by his face, he dared open his eyes and saw the clouds up ahead that signaled the silvery realm he had been thrown down from so many eons ago. His tears kept falling, faster now, washing down his cheeks and onto Eve as he landed on the heavy clouds.

"A sight I thought to never see," his brother Michael said, greeting him. His warm smile was something Lucifer hadn't seen in a very long time.

Lucifer handed his brother the limp form of Eve with a pleading look, words stuck in his throat for the first time since light first washed over the earth.

"It's alright. I have her, brother, she will be saved." Michael turned and vanished, to be replaced by another, smaller angelic being.

"We meet at last, Lucifer, or should I call you Natasha?" This woman stood only five feet tall, with long auburn hair and green eyes. Her vibrant golden wings beat slowly in the warm air.

"Jophiel, I've heard that you were promoted to archangel after I was pushed. Lucifer will do, thank you." He bowed to her and smiled at her shock. It was well known that he hated her advancement after his displacement.

"Why the name 'Natasha' in the first place, if I may ask?" Jophiel asked, turning as more angels came to stare at the prodigal son of God retuned. "Everyone has been trying to figure it out for years."

Lucifer laughed and inched closer, leaning in to whisper to her so no one else could over hear. "Spell it backward."

Jophiel cocked her head and smiled. "Ah, Satan. Clever."

Gabriel landed next to them in a rush, looking extremely worried. "Well, I see I worried for naught.

Where's Eve?" he asked as he dusted off his suit for no reason.

Before Lucifer could answer, Michael appeared in a blur with Eve at his side looking perfectly whole. Although her wings were restored, her black scales remained. "Here she is, brother." Michael bowed to Lucifer slightly, to the gasps of the gathered angels. His glowing smile showed that he did that on purpose. He then turned to Gabriel and clasped hands with the archangel. "It truly is a reunion," he said

Lucifer laughed at his brothers and took Eve's hand, hugged her to him, then held her at arm's length. "Nice scales." His smile was all that needed to be said. He looked at Michael and his face grew serious. "So, what do we do now, brother?"

"Yeah, and what about me?" Eve asked, sinking more deeply into Lucifer's embrace.

Michael laughed and waved away the serious look as he turned to dismiss the gathered host. "Now? Well, that is up to the both of you. You've both been welcomed home. Eve can lead the hunters which I hear will be repurposed, and Lucifer has a place at His feet once more."

Lucifer looked at Michael with shock. After a few seconds he composed himself once more and smiled. "But then, who would watch over the Hell down there?"

"Oh, don't worry. Father has someone in mind." Michael beckoned them both and they all vanished to the throne of God to celebrate.

Uriel walked out of the cathedral, fuming at the devil's sacrifice, and just knew that he would look bad in Father's eyes now. *And how dare Gabriel threaten me like that, I was only doing Father's work,* Uriel thought as the rain seemed to finally stop. The sun rose over the distant mountains and he breathed a sigh of contentment. *No matter, I will redeem myself when I recondition that tart.*

"Not having the best day, are you?" a seductive voice asked from behind him.

Uriel turned to see Lilith, horns out and all, sauntering towards him, her hips swaying with every step. "What do you want, demon?" he asked as he shook out his coat.

"Well, I came to see how it all played out, but I see I'm too late," Lilith said as she pouted. "How about we..."

Uriel ignored her and turned away, knowing that he had business in Heaven. He was about to unfurl his wings when the world stopped, the birds hanging ominously in the air, even Lilith was frozen, her mouth hanging open in mid sentence.

"You won't be coming home, son. Stay now and take your brothers place for the harm you have caused."

Uriel flinched at the sound of God's voice echoing in his head and felt pure despair crash down around him. Uriel fell to his knees in supplication. "No, please, Father!" Time started again and the voice was gone. It had been so long since he had truly spoken to his Father that this admonishment felt even worse.

"...grab some coffee and relax for once," Lilith finished, not realizing what just happened.

Uriel knelt there in the rising sun, kneeling in a puddle and truly knew how it must've felt for Lucifer. *No. I haven't been thrown down, that must've felt so much worse, but I'm stuck here now. Banished.* Uriel's thoughts spun, yet knowledge was always his strength. His greatest fear had finally been realized...Uriel was now the devil to a broken world. *Well, when the devil drives...* he thought getting to his feet and smiling at Lilith.

"Are you alright?" Lilith asked, just now looking around like she missed something.

"I'm fine, dear sister. Say, why don't we get that coffee. I have some plans I want to go over with you," Uriel said, bowing and taking her hand.

Appendix

People

Here is a composed list of the major—and minor—characters in these stories and a brief description of them. They are listed alphabetically and any other names they go by are listed under their main heading.

Aleksandr Cain - Son of Sandra Cain and progeny of Cain himself. Saved from the Mark of Cain when he was seven, Alek is part of a prophesy to either doom, or save the world. One of the Children of Destiny and Life partner to *Simon Rand.* He has brown hair and dark brown eyes.

Amanda Slone - Saved by the archangel of death, and family friend of the Rand's, Amanda adopted Simon Rand after the child's mother passed away. She has strawberry blond hair and deep green eyes.

Ariel - The Archangel of Nature. Ariel has deep brown wings and favors earthy colors and jeans. She has the gift of communication and can calm emotions. Ariel is the watcher of the world's cryptids and loves all animals She has long brown hair, the color of dirt, and emerald eyes.

Azrael - The Archangel of Death. Azrael has large raven black wings and dresses in ripped jeans and a leather jacket. He has been on earth for millennia and loves humanity for all their flaws. He has the gift of healing but it is not as powerful as Raphael's. He has ice-blue eyes and long raven black hair. Goes by the name *Aleksandr.*

Belial - One of the angels that fell from grace with Lucifer when he was exiled from Heaven. Belial lost his body completely in his fall and now exists as a ghost-like entity that can inhabit bodies. This Fallen angel—often called a demon in these times—possessed Marcus Brant right before the world broke. Has the power of bringing out darkest emotions in people, though not as strong as Lilith's. Also known as *Abaddon* or *Abalam*.

Cain - The First Murderer. Cain is a massive man with broad shoulders and a smile that rarely touches his eyes. Cursed by God for killing his brother Abel, Cain can never fully die, coming back from death every time, yet feeling everything. He has piercing eyes the color of wet dirt—a deep brown that seemed made of the very earth itself—and long brown hair with very tanned skin. Ancestor of Sandra and Aleksandr Cain. Goes by the name *Adam*

Evenal - Hunter angel that fell from grace after refusing to kill the Children of Destiny. She had two-tone black/white wings before she fell. Eve's skin has hardened into some sort of scales, almost like a dragon, and has turned a deep black to match her hair. She has black hair and grey eyes. Goes by the name of *Eve*.

Gabriel - The Archangel of Heralds. Gabriel was God's voice and messenger, but since coming down to earth he has been quiet in that department. Gabriel has wings that are a gorgeous two-tone white/brown and he favors white tailored suits. He has the gift of remembering anything he has seen and minor healing. He has long dirty blond hair and green eyes like liquid emeralds.

Jobe - This homeless man usually resides in a cardboard box in a park. He wears white robes with no shoes and his brown hair blends perfectly with his tanned skin. Bright eyes shine with mischief. also known as *Jesus Christ.*

Jophiel - The Archangel of Beauty. She was elevated to Archangel back when Lucifer was thrown down. Jophiel has brilliant golden wings that glint in sunlight. She has the gift of revealing one's inner light and showing them their destiny. She had long auburn hair and vibrant green eyes. Also goes by the name *Jo*.

Kalian - Hunter angel sent to bring back Evenal after she feel from heaven's grace. He has bland brown wings and was the smallest of the angels at only four feet eleven inches. He has light brown hair and blue eyes, usually keeping his hair in a pony tail. Also goes by *Kal*

Lilith - One of the angels that fell from grace with Lucifer when he was exiled from heaven. She wears black dresses cut up her legs almost to her waist. Lilith also has curling horns that spread out from her head that she grew from the burnt wing stalks on her back. Has the power to turn people's emotions to lust and carnal desire. Voice is very compulsive. Has black hair and black eyes that resemble twin pools of tar. Also known as *Hecate*.

Lucifer - The Fallen Archangel of Light. Oldest of the archangels and sat at the foot of God before the fall. He has majestic white wings and has resided on earth since the fall. He has the gift of foresight. He has blond hair, brilliant hazel eyes, and favors Armani suits, complete with silver cuff links and polished shoes He also goes by *Natasha, Satan*—though he is not overly fond of that one—and *The Morningstar.*

Marcus Brant - Private investigator from Chicago before the world broke. Born with heterochromia—mismatched eyes—he was taken by the fallen angel Belial as a host just before the calamity happened. Kept alive by the angelic force within him all these years and only looks to be sixty or so. Later used by Nergal when Belial was beaten by Lucifer. He has black hair, one green eye, and one blue eye.

Margaret Cain - Mother of Sandra Cain and Grandmother of Aleksandr Cain. Descendant of Cain the first murderer. Gravelly voice with white curly hair and glasses.

Michael - The Archangel of Battle. Michael has bright white feathered wings and usually dresses like a priest. He is the leader of the earthly angels that came down from heaven to walk among humanity and has the gift of knowing where any angel, or archangel, is at any given moment if he desires to. He has golden hair and bright blue eyes. Also goes by the name *Father Michael*

Nergal - One of the angels that fell from grace with Lucifer when he was exiled from heaven. Nergal lost his body completely in his fall and now exists as a ghost-like entity that can inhabit bodies. This Fallen angel—often called a demon in these times—possessed a demon hunting priest named Joseph right before the world broke but lost the body in the wake of destruction. Later, possessed the body of Marcus Brant after Lucifer freed it from Belial. Now in the body of a cat, thanks to Jobe. Has the power to turn luck extremely bad for anyone. Also known as Legion and acronyms of those letters for fun.

Raphael - The Archangel of Healing. Raphael was the most tender of the angelic host and felt love for every living being. Raphael has wings that are diaphanous silver and glow in the moonlight. Raphael has the gift of healing and even can raise the dead. She has long bone-white hair and silver eyes. Goes by the name of *Raina*.

Samson - The Eternal warrior. Samson was best known for his long hair, which, even now, was braided down his back. The thick, brown locks brimmed with power from an old curse, he had olive skin and the eyes of a killer.

Sandra Cain - Doctor at Mercy General in the Virginia Council States and mother to Aleksandr Cain. Descendant of the first murderer Cain. She has dirty blond hair and deep brown eyes.

Simon Rand - Seer of God and son of David and Mary Rand. African-American adopted by Amanda Slone when his mother died. One of the Children of Destiny and life-partner to *Aleksandr Cain.* He has dark skin, very short hair, and eyes like liquid chocolate.

Uriel - The Archangel of Knowledge. Uriel has glorious silver wings and dresses in a trench coat and hat. He has the gift of foresight—though it is not as powerful as Lucifer's—and can see patterns while on earth that he is learning to influence. He has light brown hair and grey eyes.

Places

These are just some of the places that are featured in this anthology of stories. There are many more places that thrive and others that fell into darkness, as well as the many other countries around the world.

Field State of Oklahoma - This abandoned state of empty farms and fields of wild flowers serves as a reminder of how the world used to be. Abandoned when the economy started to collapse, this state offered almost nothing to the people left to rebuild. The rare town or village can still be found along broken highways and back roads alike. These dwindling vestiges of human gatherings are mostly populated by the stubborn and desperate, yet they are often kind and willing to help others in need. The one thing this state does have in abundance is rusty farming equipment and miles of over grown fields.

New Colorado - New Colorado is one of the most peaceful places in this new time. High walls surround a massive area from Boulder all the way to the national parks. Most people live in the forests now, making their homes among the sturdy trees and branches, as well as among the forest floor. Very few prefer to live in the rebuilt city anymore, however, as it reminds them of the way things used to be. New Colorado is a place of recreation and commerce, having the market on skiing, hiking, and tourism that only the New England City States could compete with.

New Dallas - This massive city state was one of the more economically sound places in the new world, being kept safe by the Rangers of old. They had built high stone walls when the worst came down, and limited entrance to refugees. This caused some rioting and the violence that ensued was some of the bloodiest in the new world. Though it was a hard call, in the end the city state prospered and grew—with many of its residents filling the ranks of the Rangers to replace their fallen numbers. The city is run by the head of the Ranger's, a dictator with absolute power over the city.

New England City States - The individual states of New Hampshire, Vermont, Maine, and Massachusetts, came together after the catastrophe and set aside all differences to create a safe haven for the people. They built a wall around their borders and rebuilt their cities towards the central part of the large area, letting nature take back the edges. These edges are still populated by small towns here and there—folk too stubborn to leave their homes or others that just love living among nature. The massive forests are patrolled by packs of Hunters, the official guard of the N.E.C.S. These Hunters are trained in military tactics and carry state of the art weapons as well as camouflage armor.

New Seattle - This city state was lucky during the calamity, as most everything west of the city went under when California was lost. They survived and built a massive seawall, sheltering the city and surrounding Mercer Island Retreat, which now served as the home of the wealthy and powerful. The suburbs of New Seattle filled with refugees from the city itself and even the mountains to the east boast more towns in the new world than ever in history.

Old California Island - When the world broke, the fault line under California shattered and sunk most of the state, flooding the major cities-if not completely submerging them. thousands of miles of land slid into the ocean as the quakes destroyed most of the civilized areas. Millions tried to escape the devastation wrought by the calamity and the ensuing chaos was the worse in all the country. When it had all settled, what was left was a large island with waterlogged streets and wooden walkways. The people that remained built what they could and salvaged from the wreckage. Tourists now flock here to see the underwater buildings and statues that remain in the crystal-clear waters.

Old Chicago - When the calamity struck, the entire city of Chicago was torn apart by high winds and quakes. Most of the tall buildings had fallen down at once, creating massive piles of rubble and burying the smaller structures. Streets were jammed with chunks of stone and overturned cars, making travel almost impossible through the wreckage. Now, people live in hovels and shelters made from the debris and bow down to warlords that carved out sections for their home bases.

Old Detroit - When the calamity broke the world, many places of civilization fell quickly due to the damage and loss of life. This city fell to looting and riots more than anything else and was now home to gang wars and rivalries. The young and reckless are recruited for the bangers' power moves and most everyone else stays hidden in their homes The brave souls that do dare come out tread carefully—mostly under the cover of darkness—to scavenge for what little supplies they can find, with a brave few hitting the depots of the bangers.

Old Miami - Old Miami is a rarity, as most of the surrounding cities have been flooded when the world broke. Here, at the tip of the state, the water receded and the survivors scrambled to erect some kind of wall to keep the high tide from submerging them completely. It had worked, somehow, but now the Warlords controlled everything. These warlords deal in weapons and drugs to keep the people in line, mostly using fear and violence to keep them in line. No one dares venture out at night unless they have business with a dealer.

Ruined Nebraska - This entire state went up in flames when the world broke—some of the fires are still burning to this day—and no one knows why. There are theories, of course, but with the world in chaos, no one really cares enough to find out. Some theorize that it is oil fields that caused it, while others speculate that the old government had secret propane reserves hidden when the economy was at its worst. These days most of the places that aren't on fire are desolate, empty, rural towns and conglomerate villages just trying to survive.

Ruins of Phoenix - Arizona had been hit the worst, fallout destroying most of the state; Phoenix was the only thing that barely survived—if you wanted to call this surviving. The people that made this ruined city their home are scarred and broken; most of the children born now have deformities due to radiation and chemical pollution. The immense pine forests that once decorated the state are all but gone, with only a fraction of the great trees surviving. Some people are rumored to have taken up residence in the sparse grove of trees, yet no one has ever come back to tell; all who venture there disappear.

The Virginia Council States - Here, the remnants of Virginia, West Virginia, and the tattered remains of Maryland came together and rebuilt, favoring hospitals over anything else. They are now known as having the best hospitals in Northern America. They also have some of the only schools left to teach medicine outside of the N.E.C.S.

About the author

Born in the usual way, author Michael D. Nadeau found fantasy at the age of eight with Dungeons & Dragons. He loved being different people as well as casting magic. By High school he discovered his love for reading thanks to a teacher. She fed his thirst for books by bringing her own collections from home and lending them to him, even buying one towards the end of her class. He has now read hundreds of fantasy books, living in each of their worlds along with the characters. After awhile he started creating his own worlds for his games with friends. Cities, gods, ancient and terrible beings and histories...then he would burn them all down.

He is the author of the Lythinall series: *The Darkness Returns* book 1, *The Darkness Within* book 2, *The Darkness Falls* Book 3, *Dragon Caller; Rise of the archmage* book1, *Dragon Master; Rise of the Archmage* book 2, and *Tales from Lythinall*—an anthology. He also has several stories in Eerie River Publishing anthologies, as well as writing on his own.